All Things Cat

Short stories to warm the cat lover's heart.

by

Elaine Faber

Elk Grove Publications

All Things Cat

Short stories to warm the cat lover's heart.

Published by Elk Grove Publications

© 2017 by Elaine Faber

ISBN-13: 978-1-940781-20-4

A portion of the proceeds from the sale of this book are donated to support feline rescue projects.

These stories are works of fiction. Names, characters, places, and incidents either are the product of the author's imagination or are used for editorial purposes. Any resemblance to actual events, locales, organizations, or persons, living or dead, is entirely coincidental and beyond the intent of either the author or publisher.

Cover photo *Truffie* © Elaine Faber

Cover layout and book formatting: Julie Williams, juliewilliams.us
Printed in the United States of America

Contents

Introduction

From the beginning of recorded time, cats have shared our lives, gained our trust, protected our harvests and warmed our beds.

Over the years, cats have been both revered and reviled. Currently, millions of American families are "owned" by a cat. (If you are reading this book, it is a fair bet that you are also "owned" by a cat.) Many videos on Facebook and YouTube are about the behaviors, antics, and expressions of cats.

It seemed evident at this time, that a book of short stories exclusively about cats would have wide acceptance.

The following twenty-one stories range from humorous to heartrending, featuring cats from diverse walks of life and varying periods of time.

Some are first-person accounts, written by anonymous felines. Likely, these authors had no intention of sharing their innermost thoughts with the world. These stories will amaze and endear readers to their hidden thoughts, fears, and insecurities.

Other stories illustrate how cats affect, impact or enrich our lives through their contributions or companionship.

All the stories, written by Elaine Faber, curious tales of fact and fiction, were inspired by a plethora of situations, news events, contest prompts, holidays, and the like. Also included are excerpts from Faber's novels, *Black Cat's Legacy, Black Cat and the Lethal Lawyer*, and *Mrs. Odboddy – Hometown Patriot*.

Dead Bush Poker

ead Bush, where I grew up, is a small town in the center of
Texas. I'm a fine figure of a cat, though some would say,
somewhat on the portly side. The compliment is validated by
the roaming tomcat that comes through town every spring. Up until
now, I haven't given him a tumble, but I'm thinking that next spring
might be a fine time to start a family.

Dead Bush sports three saloons, a general store, the bank, one
church without a steeple, a blacksmith shop and another motely hotel-
like establishment such as nice folks shouldn't talk about in mixed
company. Modern wooden slat sidewalks were added this spring
in deference to the request of those specific ladies who live in the
aforementioned establishment.

On Founder's Day, the local farmer's wives bake pies and hams
and sweet potatoes for a giant banquet and sponsor a square dance
out behind the Blacksmith's shop. Bright and early this morning,
neighboring farmers trickled into town with planks and sawhorses for
the long tables needed for the annual banquet.

Long about 10:00 AM, several soldiers still wearing raggedy Civil
War uniforms, rode into Dead Bush on horses that looked like they'd
been rode hard and put away wet. The soldiers commenced to drink
and gamble and ordered steak dinners at the Dry Spell Saloon where,
among other things, such entertainment and libation is provided.

I've made my home in the back of the saloon where I sleep on a
stack of burlap sacks, ever since the town sheriff found me, the lone
survivor of a wagon train massacred by a tribe of wild Indians. Shorty,
the barkeep saves left-overs for me from the day's leavings. That,

added to my hunting prowess, fares me well in the eats department. According to the regulars at the saloon, who sort of adopted me as a mascot, cats are almighty scarce and considerable valuable in this part of the country. A number of local farmers have offered Shorty big bucks for me, beings as cats can keep a barnyard free of varmints. There are some cowpokes from the big cities who haul cats in their saddlebags to small farming towns, assured of a quick sale and a $20 gold piece.

Well, seems these soldiers what came to town with their long rifles and powder horns sat and drank well past noon. When I wandered through the saloon, it caused quite a stir amongst the gamblers. One of the soldiers took a hankerin' to buy me, having heard about big money being paid for cats up the river. Shorty declined, saying I couldn't be sold since I was a free spirit and didn't belong to nobody.

As the gambling and drinking progressed, the soldier plied Shorty with enough palaver and drink that they cajoled him into a game of poker with me as the stakes.

I sat near the potbelly stove, preening my whiskers, somewhat amused by the stupidity of these humans what thought they could buy and sell another living creature. Didn't the Civil War just disprove that notion? The scent of barbequed chicken wafting through the open door caught my attention and I left the fools to their folly.

I ambled out the door and down the sidewalk, past the wooden cigar Indian in front of the general store and rounded the nearest banquet table laden with food. The oldest six of Mrs. Barnwhistle's nine children cornered me straight away and near strangled the life out of me with their stroking and clutching, shifting me from child to child, chucking under my chin. I've learned to put up with the nonsense of children as long as they don't pull my tail, as it puts their mothers in a fair mood when you allow such behavior. They get such a kick out of seeing their child all jollified, they usually smile and offer me a pinch of chicken or slice of bread and butter. If things get out of hand after such a juvenile mauling, I can always get away and find a quiet place to lick off the sticky jam or mud clinging to my furs.

Hearing raucous laughter coming from the saloon, I felt it prudent to check on the doings, as it seemed my future as mascot at the Dry Spell Saloon was dependent on the turn of their cards.

Four players hunched over the poker table, cards fanned in their hands, splashes of liquor pooling on the table, empty glasses lined up in front of each man. Shorty's chips were considerably fewer than the other three. Holding on to the Dry Spell Saloon mascot didn't look too promising.

The height of Shorty's chips rose and fell as the afternoon wore on. I sat on a nearby table, commiserating with Mr. Casper, a gray-haired old codger who operated a small gold claim in a nearby river. Shorty always ended up with most of Mr. Casper gold, in exchange for liquor. The old man was a fool, but he didn't smell quite as bad as the other miners, as being tipsy most of the time, Mr. Casper fell in the river more often than most, washing away some of his natural man-stink.

In the late afternoon, the ladies announced that their Founder's Day supper was served for any who cared to partake. The saloon emptied except for the four poker players, who found it harder and harder to sit straight in their chairs. Heads lolled and cards tumbled from their hands. When they poured another drink, more whiskey landed on the floor than in their glasses. Never in the history of Dead Bush had such a game gone on for so long or the stakes so roundly coveted. I was, indeed, a prize worthy of much effort and consternation.

Eventually, Smitty Rosenblatt passed out. George Waddlebaker went broke. Shorty hung in there, though blurry eyed and slumped shouldered, he continued to fight for his meezer. Poor Shorty. He looked ready to throw in the towel.

Seeing the inevitable handwriting on the wall, I slipped out the front door and headed out onto the prairie, intending on being absent from town for the next four or five days.

An occasional trip away from home is always revitalizing to one's health. I couldn't see no sense being around when Shorty went broke and the soldier attempted to claim his prize. After all, a cat is a free spirit, don't belong to nobody and shouldn't be won in no poker game. Besides, I didn't plan to be strung to the back of a saddle in a burlap sack until the old soldier found a farmer with a rat-filled barn and a $20 gold piece.

I'm the only cat worth its salt in Dead Bush, and I intend to keep it that way…at least until next spring when that tomcat, Tom, comes back to town.

Bubbles Baubles

He stood in the dark hallway. A thrill of anticipation plunged down his spine. Every detail carefully planned. Kill her, run down the back stairs, drive to the motel and pretend disbelief when he heard of his wife's unfortunate demise.

He opened Myrtle's bedroom door, rushed across the room, swung the flashlight to her temple. Myrtle's blood splashed across the sheets and pooled beneath her head. He stood over her as the crimson liquid oozed down her wrinkled cheek and dripped from the bed to the floor, drip . . . drip . . . drip . . . .

Herbert stifled a yawn and opened his eyes. His bedroom furniture looked ghostly in the breaking dawn. His stomach seized at the memory of Myrtle's blood-soaked head. *My God, this time I really did it. I killed her. I need to get out of here before—*

"Herbert! Herbert! Can't you hear me? I'm calling you."

His heart plummeted. He sat up, rubbing his eyes. Fingers of sweat crept down his back at the sound of her voice.

"I need to go to the bathroom. Come and help me."

Still alive. He sighed and staggered from his warm bed. When would he have the courage to kill her? He stumbled to Myrtle's room and threw back the covers.

Too late. She lay in a puddle of wet sheets.

"Now, see what *you* made me do," she snapped. "Why can't you come when I call? Bring me dry clothes and run my bath. You can change the sheets while I bathe."

Myrtle shrieked when Bubbles jumped on the bed. "Get that damn cat off my bed."

Herbert shooed Bubbles off the bed and helped Myrtle pull off her wet gown. Flabby layers of fat bulged beneath her sagging breasts. Blotchy skin on her skinny legs reminded him of chicken legs draining in the sink. He shuddered.

"I'll run your bath, all right," he muttered filling the tub. "Maybe I'll hold your ugly head under the water until you turn blue. Folks will think you slipped in the tub." His mouth twisted in a smirk.

"Meow"

Herbert turned as Bubbles waddled into the bathroom.

"Hey, Bubbles." Herbert buried his face in her long dark fur. He drew a ragged breath and swallowed a lump in his throat. "If it wasn't for you... I can't go on like this much longer."

The cat wiggled from his grasp.

Herbert sighed and returned to help Myrtle from her bed into the tub.

While Myrtle napped later that morning, Herbert drove to Pet Club. He placed bags of Friskies and kitty litter into his basket, and then pushed his cart to the display of animal collars. He glanced up and down the aisle. No one was watching. Just what he needed–a pink cat collar covered with clear rhinestones.

Perspiration beaded his brow as he hurried through the checkout stand.

On the way home, he concentrated on self-talk. This time, he wouldn't chicken out. This time, he'd go through with the plan. While Myrtle slept, he'd open the safe and remove the diamonds her father left her. She had hidden the safe's combination between the pages of D.H. Lawrence's erotic novel, *Lady Chatterley's Lover*. Now wasn't that a joke?

How often they had quarreled about those damn diamonds. How often had he begged her to sell them, but she refused? He was just a slave, that's what he was, but not for long. This time he'd do it.

Tiptoeing into the house, he found she had fallen asleep. He slipped past her bed, located the book and retrieved the combination.

Then he quietly opened the safe and removed the diamonds. Once back in the kitchen, he used jeweler's pliers to replace the rhinestones in the cat collar with Myrtle's diamonds, and clamped down the prongs.

Ah. A perfect fit.

Sneaking back into the bedroom, he placed the rhinestones back into the safe, spun the dial, and slipped the combination into the book on the shelf. *Pshew!*

"Here, Bubbles. Here, kitty, kitty," he called, once back in the kitchen where he found the cat lapping water at her bowl. "There now, my beauty," he said, as he fastened the diamond-filled collar around her neck. "Aren't you the pretty one?"

Bubbles twisted to lick at the foreign object around her neck.

Next, he made reservations for Friday night at a motel in downtown Sacramento.

"Herbert! Herbert."

His blood ran cold. His stomach roiled. Oh, how he hated her. "Myrtle!"

"Bring me another cup of coffee. Don't forget to put it in the microwave. It's only lukewarm from the pot. If I've told you once, I've told you a hundred times. You're just worthless."

He slipped the rat poison into Myrtle's coffee. It swirled in a series of delightful designs as it sank through the amber liquid and settled in a pool in the bottom of the cup. He crept up the stairs. "Here's your coffee, sweetheart. Drink it all down like a good girl."

Myrtle drank and within a minute, her face grew deathly pale and she writhed in pain. Her skinny fingers clutched at her throat as she gagged, shuddered and died in hideous agony. He stood over her body as the blood trickled from her twisted mouth and dripped onto the floor, drip . . . drip . . . drip . . . .

"Herbert? Did you hear me? I'm still waiting."

Herbert jerked. Back from his reverie, he poured the coffee, placed it in the microwave and set the dial for two minutes. Maybe she'd burn her ugly mouth when she drank it.

What fun it had been to imagine new ways to commit murder. But he'd finally settled on a foolproof plan and put it into motion. He smiled as he carried the coffee up the stairs.

When she fell asleep that night, Herbert slipped out the door, eased the car from the garage and drove to the neighborhood pub where he engaged in conversation with the local drunk, Chuck. After three beers and several trips to the boy's room within half an hour, the neon lights spelling *Beer and Wine* began to slither across the bar's dark window. Herbert blinked to bring the letters into focus. Now, he'd pretend to be drunk and put on a pretty convincing show. It didn't take much effort.

"I could have me a little book store," Herbert whined, touching his handkerchief to his forehead. "But no, the old lady won't sell her blasted diamonds. What good are diamonds locked up in the safe?" His hand went to his eyes as though concealing tears. He peeked through his fingers. Was Chuck buying it? Indeed, he looked quite interested.

"In the safe, ya' say?" Chuck tossed back his drink. "Yer' right. Diamonds don't do nobody much good there in the library safe."

"*Nah*, not in the library." Herbert picked up his beer and took a swig. "Safe's in the bedroom, behind the picture over the stereo, that's where she keeps them." He sighed. "And, she doesn't even trust me with the combination. She tried to hide it from me. But I figured it out, all right. 36-24-36. Now, who does she think she's kidding?"

Herbert slid his gaze toward the bartender, making sure he'd remember their conversation. Chuck would be the perfect patsy for Myrtle's murder.

Herbert choked back a sob. "I'm going to leave her, that's what I'm going to do. Friday night, right after she goes to sleep...at eight o'clock." *Maybe a little overkill? Nah!*

Chuck nodded, his face the picture of sorrow. "Friday night, ya' say? Here, pal, have another drink. You'll feel better."

Herbert's car wandered from side to side as he drove away from the bar, satisfied with his performance and in no hurry to get home.

He tiptoed up the stairs to where she lay sleeping. His fingers twitched as he reached for her scrawny neck. He clutched her throat and squeezed until his fingers ached and her face turned a ripe shade of purple. She gasped. Her thrashing knocked her water glass from the nightstand. At last, she lay still. He stood over her body as water flowed across the nightstand and dripped onto the floor, drip . . . drip . . . drip . . . .

"Herbert? Is that you? Where have you been? You've been gone for over an hour. I'm lying here in pain, as if you cared. Bring me my medicine. And, be quick about it."

Myrtle. Still awake.

Herbert no sooner entered her bedroom, than Bubbles jumped on the bed and pushed her head under his hand. He stroked her back, pausing for a moment as his fingers passed over the diamonds on the collar. Not long now... "Come on, Bubbles. Myrtle needs her pain medicine."

On Friday afternoon, Herbert sat in the library, his heart pounding, reading a magazine. He glanced at his watch. 3:00 PM. Any minute now, she'd be yowling for her coffee—

"Herbert. Bring me some coffee. You know I like my afternoon coffee. If you weren't so lazy, you'd bring me a cup before I have to ask, but you don't care if I lie up here and die of thirst, do you?"

He stood and grinned at Bubbles. "Time to get the show on the road. Here we go." He carried his packed suitcase into Myrtle's room.

"Where do you think you're going?" She scooted up against the headboard, oddly needing no assistance. She had required help to sit up every morning for the past three months.

"I'm leaving you." Herbert smirked. "Get yourself another coffee boy. I've had enough."

"You can't leave." Myrtle's eyes grew wide. "Who will take care of me?"

"In Clark Gable's words from *Gone With the Wind*, 'I don't give a flying fig.'" Herbert turned toward the door.

"That's not what he said, you fool," Myrtle called after him. "He said, 'frankly my dear, I don't give a damn.'"

"And frankly, my dear, neither do I." Herbert hurried into the hallway where he turned to wink at Bubbles. "Don't worry. I'll see you real soon." He scampered down the stairs grinning like a schoolboy just let out of school for summer recess. "Bye-bye."

Herbert drove to a busy shopping center in Rancho Cordova where he paid cash for a box of plastic gloves and a large flashlight, then on to the Starlight Motel, a block from the Crest Theater. He registered, paid with a credit card and asked for the receipt. "Can you tell me where I could find the nearest movie house?" The expression on his face was one of pure innocence.

The clerk handed Herbert a printout from the Crest Theater. "They're playing Hitchcock movies at the Crest all month. Just down the street. Tonight's movie is, *The Birds*."

He'd seen *The Birds* a dozen times and knew the story line well. He'd read about the Hitchcock movies in *The Sacramento Bee*. "Sounds like fun. Thanks for the information." He sashayed out the door, waving the brochure.

At 8:00 PM, he drove to the theater, bought a ticket and found a seat in a dark corner. At 8:50 PM, he left his coat and hat in the seat and stole out the back door, leaving it slightly ajar. He hurried back to his South Sacramento neighborhood, stopped a block from his house on a dark street, crept down the street and tiptoed through the backyard of the house backing up to his house and climbed the fence. He crept across the patio and used a screwdriver to break the lock on the back door. *This time I'm doing it.* His mouth felt as dry as a cardboard hatbox.

A glance at his watch showed 9:20 P.M. She should be asleep. It was so clear in his mind, how he'd do it, just as he'd imagined a hundred times. *He tiptoed across the room toward the lump in the bed and swung the flashlight down onto her forehead. He heard the crunch as the bones of her forehead gave way beneath the blow. He stood over her body, as the blood poured from her temple, down her ugly cheek and then dripped from the edge of the bed onto the floor, drip . . . drip*

. . . drip . . . .

Open the safe, take the envelope with the rhinestones and sneak back to the movie house. He should arrive about the time the birds attacked the Bodega Bay residents. Back at the motel after the movie, he'd tell the clerk all about the movie. Between the credit card receipts, the movie ticket and the motel clerk's story, he had the perfect alibi for Myrtle's estimated time of death.

Tomorrow, pretending he'd lost his key, he and his neighbor with the spare would discover the tragedy together. Chuck would be arrested for Myrtle's murder and the theft of the diamonds. Herbert would file a claim for Myrtle's life insurance and for the stolen diamonds. In six months, he'd be rich.

Satisfied with his plan, Herbert crept up the stairs and stood outside her bedroom door, his heart pounding so loud he was sure he'd wake her, the flashlight clutched in his sweaty hand. He put his ear to the door and listened. His forehead prickled with moisture.

Silence.

She's asleep. This time I'll do it for sure. He reached a shaking hand toward the door handle, and then charged into the room, the flashlight raised.

Bubbles lay sprawled across the pillows on Myrtle's empty bed.

The picture over the stereo drooped at a 45 degree angle.

The door of the safe hung askew. He crossed the room and peeked inside.

Empty except for an envelope with his name scrawled across the front.

Herbert dropped the flashlight on the bed, ripped open the envelope and held the letter in the beam of light.

Dear Herbert:

I'm tired of pretending. I'm perfectly well. You are such a fool. Look how long you waited on me hand and foot. You aren't going to leave me, I'm leaving you. With Daddy's diamonds, I can live like a queen. Good-bye, sucker. Myrtle

Herbert stared at Myrtle's empty bed. Bubbles stretched and the light from the flashlight glinted off her collar, casting a rainbow of colors across the far wall.

She's gone. I'm free. And I didn't have to kill her.

Herbert laughed until tears rolled down his cheeks. No more fetching coffee. No more changing wet sheets. No more dragging Myrtle's flabby body across the bedroom into the tub. He fell onto the bed, reached for the cat and stroked her head. "We're free, Bubbles. We can go anywhere...Do anything we want."

He lay there for a minute, feeling his pounding heart begin to quiet. He stared at the empty safe for a long moment. What *did* he want to do for the rest of his life?

He had no friends except Bubbles, and no hobbies. The only pleasure in his life was plotting Myrtle's murder and now even that pleasure was gone. He grabbed Bubbles and clutched her to his chest, tears pricking his eyes.

A rush of panic gripped his throat. "What am I going to do now?" A wave of nausea swept through his stomach. "Wait. As soon as she figures out the diamonds are fakes, she'll come back." The realization hit him like a bucket of ice water.

Everything would be just like before. She'd shriek for incessant cups of coffee. She'd have him fetching and carrying until he'd think his back would break. She'd criticize and berate him. Life would become even more unbearable than before because she'd know he switched the diamonds for rhinestones. *She'll never forgive me.* Terror clutched his heart.

And then he saw the words, as clear as if written on a giant billboard stretching across Arco Arena at a Kings' basketball game. *You'll have to kill her.* A warm tingle flowed from his toes to his fingertips. He shivered with anticipation.

She'd be sleeping. He'd take a knife from the kitchen drawer and sneak up the stairs. He'd creep across the room until he stood over her bed, and then he'd plunge the knife again and again into her heart. Blood would squirt up and across the duvet and splash onto the nightstand where it would wick into the crocheted doily, then drip over the edge, drip . . . drip . . . drip . . . .

He smiled. He had no choice. This time, he'd have to do it.

Previously printed in *Capitol Crimes Anthology*, 2013.

Does God Love Cats?

I love my cat, Truffie. She's a gift of joy in my life. Every day, she makes me smile. She loves me unconditionally, even when I'm not wearing lipstick or my hair is a mess. She loves me when I'm grumpy or had a bad day. She even loves me when I accidentally step on her tail.

There was a day that Truffie stopped eating. She lost weight. We took her to the vet twice. Though we racked up $600 in medical bills, the vet's words held no reassurance, "All the lab tests and x-rays are normal. I don't know what's wrong with her. Maybe we could—"

"No," I said. "I can't afford to spend any more money. Not if we don't even know what's wrong or how to fix it."

Five days had passed since she became ill. If something didn't change soon, there was no hope for her. I took her home. I forced eye droppers full or water down her throat every few hours. She still wouldn't eat. She had a fever. None of the medicine the vet had prescribed seemed to help.

I began to wonder. *Does God care that Truffie is sick?*

Sure, we know He cares about our health and our finances and foreign affairs and protecting the troops fighting in far-away places. But does God really care if my cat is sick? Would He take time from His busy schedule of healing folks and finding work for the unemployed, and protecting our troops and trying to make the *Washington swamp* solve our problems to heal a cat just because I asked? You see, I've prayed about all those things for a while now, but Truffie's fever? *Does He really care? Do I dare pray and expect God to heal her?*

I asked my pastor, "Do you think God cares when our pets are sick? Would it help to pray for Truffie?" He told me that on a certain day, people bring their animals to the Catholic Church to be blessed, but he couldn't think of a Bible verse that specifically says God heals pets, especially cats.

I searched the Bible in hopes I'd find something to prove God cared about the animals and would answer our prayers when they're sick. Matthew reminds us...*Are not two sparrows sold for a penny? Yet not one of them will fall to the ground outside your Father's care. (Matthew 10:20 NIV)* Sparrows... Cats... Not quite the same, but if He cares about birds, it stands to reason that He cares about cats too.

We're all familiar with God's blessings and promises. We know He gives us everything we *need*. Our home... Our loved ones... A job–well, most of us have a job, or we had one, before they downsized the company, and now some of us have unemployment. But not many of us are going hungry or sleeping in the streets, so even in our adversity, God supplies our needs. But that didn't answer my question. Would it help if I ask Him to heal my cat?

I searched the scriptures for more about prayer and faith. *Ask and it will be given to you. (Matthew 7:7 NIV).* Was that the key? It went on to say that faith the size of the mustard seed could even move mountains. *For truly I say to you. If you have faith like a grain of mustard seed, you will say to this mountain, 'Move from here to there' and it will move and nothing will be impossible. (Matthew 17:20NIV)* That sounded promising. And lastly...*how much more will the Father in Heaven give good gifts to those (his children) who ask Him. (Matthew 7:11NIV)*

Now, we were getting somewhere. The Bible teaches us that it's a matter of having faith when we pray, not the specifics of what we pray about.

What have I got to lose? So I prayed for Truffie. "Lord, you know how much I love her. You know how much joy she gives me and You know how it would grieve me to lose her. I'm calling on Your promise, *Ask and it will be given....* I place this little cat in Your loving hands, Lord, and ask You to heal her and raise her up again. I have faith that she will be healed because You've promised…"

Now, I'm not going to tell you that lightning surrounded my head or that the Heavens opened and God's voice rang out, "Truffie. Rise up and walk," but the next day, Truffie started to eat. Her mood brightened. She purred. She was on her way. She would recover.

I know that God cares for our cats and dogs and rabbits and horses and all our pets. Not because there's a specific verse in the Bible that says so, but because we love them and He loves us…enough to want our joy to be complete. He promises that if we ask and have faith, we can move mulberry trees into the sea, or move mountains from here to there, or maybe it's all about teaching us to take all our cares to the Lord, no matter how big or small and knowing He will hear and answer.

Truffie was eight years old this spring and has never been sick another day in her life. Truffie is living proof. God answered my prayer, and yes, I'm convinced.

God loves cats.

Previously published in *Inspire Victory*, 2014.

Esme, the Ship's Cat

*This story is a spin-off from Thumper's memories from my novel, **Black Cat's Legacy**; all cats have their ancestors' memories. Certain things trigger those memories. Esme was one of Thumper's ancestors.*

On a particular day in May, 1789, as a metal bucket crashed to the ground inches away from her nose, Esme snatched a small fish from the display case.

"Scram! Witch from Hell! Be gone, I say, and don't come back."

Esme raced away from the wrath of the fishmonger. She slinked behind barrels for a fair distance, and then stopped to eat her stolen fish.

After sweeping her pink raspy tongue over each sticky foot and across her furry ears and down the side of her thin black face, she carefully cleaned each white whisker, repeating the process until every trace of fish smell was gone. Esme licked her shoulders and down her back, finishing up with the delicate area around her nether parts until her ebony body glistened in the bright morning sunlight. Having satisfied her hunger and completed her grooming, she curled within the center of a coiled rope and fell asleep.

For a time, Esme slept soundly, lost in tranquil blackness until sounds from the neighborhood cut through the darkness. The cat's eyes blinked open to survey her surroundings.

Near the box where she slumbered, oxen trudged the street, hauling wagonloads of goods from nearby towns. A drunken sailor staggered down the road, clutching a goatskin wine bag slung over one shoulder. He paused near the cat, uncorked the cap and lifted it to his lips. Wine spilled down his chin onto the front of his leather jerkin. He recorked the bag, tossed it onto his back, and staggered toward the dock where the colorful sails of a frigate billowed in the breeze. The sound of the flapping sails triggered Esme's memories; some pleasant and others, not so much.

Ships did not leave the harbor until a competent ship's cat was on board. Without a skilled ratter, the ship could be overrun with rats and disease was sure to follow. Esme was known for her reputation as an experienced ratter and was much sought after by ships' captains. If there was to be an ocean voyage in her future, she intended to select a ship that assured a pleasant journey. It mattered not whether it was a legitimate merchant ship or a pirate vessel. A clean ship with good food and kind sailors was more important than its legitimacy. But she was always alert, lest she be shanghaied onto a ship so overrun with rats that even an expert ratter could not control.

Off to the right of the harbor was a ship that she wished to avoid at all cost.

Off to the left, however, the bright red sails of a pirate ship caught her attention. Her gaze followed the steps of a sailor as he played a reed flute and danced a jig while his companions clapped and stomped to the music. The sound of laughter floated across the harbor. This was the kind of ship she would choose, given her choice.

Her attention strayed for only a moment as she twisted backward to scratch at an elusive flea. In that instant, a sack dropped over her body. Her world went dark and the air around her head reeked of rancid oats.

"Gottcha, you little she-devil. I'll be spendin' me gold tonight when the Cappin' sees ya'. I heared yer' the best ratter around. Cappin'll be mighty pleased."

The sailor staggered up the gangplank with the bulging sack slung over his back. He flung his prize into a dark hold on board his ship and slammed the deck lid.

Esme clawed open the sack in the hold stacked with boxes and bales. She heard a scratching sound in the corner and smelled the unmistakable odor of *rat*. As her eyes adjusted to the dim light, she spied the varmint on top of a bale in the corner.

Her left ear twitched, as with every nerve taunt, she calculated the distance, the elevation, the required thrust. She leaped. In an instant, her teeth sank through the rat's neck. The disgusting thing lay dead on the bale. One down, Were there more? The dark hold was silent. To find a rat almost immediately upon boarding the ship meant it was surely overrun with vermin. Was she trapped aboard for the duration?

As the long hours passed, her stomach gnawed with hunger and thirst. She was determined that only at the brink of starvation would she eat the wretched rat crawling with lice and fleas.

Esme blinked in the sudden brightness when the hatch screeched open and a shaggy head appeared in the square above her head.

"Hey, cat, air' ye' hungry? Cappin' says I otter' feed ye." The man held out a chunk of bread. "Where air ye, cat?"

Esme hunkered in the shadow of a box. Escape was now or never. Determined not to stay on the rat-infested vessel for the duration of the voyage, she crouched and leapt toward the crack of sunshine that spelled freedom. Her toes caught the lip of the deck and she hung suspended for a moment, and then pulled herself upward, her back feet scrabbling, until her body was on the deck.

Suddenly realizing that he was about to lose his prize, the sailor slammed down the lid, catching the end of her tail.

Esme shrieked in pain, clawing the air as the lid of the deck nearly sliced through her tail, two inches from the end. Frantic to be free, she pulled with all her strength. In agonizing pain, the last bit of her tail muscle and skin tore away. She raced across the deck, leaving a trail of blood as she barreled down the gangplank and through the town. Finally overcome with exhaustion, and overwhelmed with pain, she collapsed behind a pile of wood, her body heaving, eyes dilated, her tail throbbing. She licked the stub until the bleeding stopped. Trembling and dizzy from loss of blood, she slept.

Esme lay behind the pile of wood for a full day, feverish, weakened by hunger, thirst and pain, nursing the stub of her tail.

"What's this? Air' ye ailin' there, cat?'"

Esme woke to the soothing voice and lifted her head. She tried to pull away from the gentle hand that touched her. In such need, both physically and emotionally, she could not reject the kindness and sympathy in his touch. "Poor thing, let me look at ye.'" Esme purred as the sailor reached behind the boxes and gathered her in his arms.

On board the pirate ship, he gently washed her wound, applied a healing salve and fed her spoonsful of egg and milk. Within an hour, strengthened by the nourishment, Esme held up her head.

"Ye'll be missin' part a' yer' tail, but I doubt it be keepin' ye' from yer' duties," the captain said, stroking the cat's head. "Townsfolk declare she be lucky and the best ratter around. If she lives, we'll be blessed with a safe journey."

"She live, all right," said the First Mate. "I'll make sure a' that."

The pirate ship sailed, Esme healed and soon made friends among the bored crew. Jealously, they rivalled for her attention and gloated when she favored one above the other.

"She be wavin' her flag to me this fine morning. I think she be favorin' me most this trip," a sailor called to his friend.

"*Nah.* She be sleepin' in me bunk last night. She favors me most," his friend replied, giving his mate a shove.

"That's a lie. She follered' me to the mess last night. She knows I be the one what gives her treats. She favors me." The scruffy pirate struck his rival, roared an oath and flung his friend to the floor where they struggled, kicking and punching.

Yanking the men to their feet by their collars, the captain said, "If I be seein' any more fightin' amongst ye' over that there cat, I'll fling her overboard. Do ye' hear me? I'll allow no fightin' aboard this ship. There's time enough for fightin' when we come upon a pretty vessel loaded with fine goods askin' fer the takin'. I'll not have ye' laid up with a busted jaw from fightin' ore a blasted cat."

Esme sat atop the captain's deck, preening her short black hair, pretending not to understand the situation below. The look in her eyes was as impish as a devil from hell. This trip couldn't have turned out better. There weren't many rats on board; just enough to keep her entertained on a dull afternoon. She had the ship's crew twisted around one of the six toes on her front foot. Crewmembers idolized and sought her favor with attention and snacks. The weather was fine and her tail only ached a little on foggy days. Life was good, indeed.

As the trip progressed, the pirate ship attacked frigates on their way from Spain to New England loaded with tea, fine linens, jewelry and chests of gold coins. When the merchants complained bitterly to the King of Spain, he sent war ships along the trade route, determined to put a stop to the pirate raids.

One morning, Esme slept on a water barrel near the rail of the pirate ship. A light breeze fluttered the sails. Fog hung thick over the sea, creating poor visibility.

The crew had slept late, having seized a merchant ship the day before and celebrated late into the night, drinking from casks of rum taken from the captured ship. Only a minimal watch crew was awake on deck and most of them were nodding at their post.

Hidden by the surrounding fog off the port side, the King's ship attacked, sending a cannon ball crashing into the unsuspecting pirate ship. Water gushed through a hole in the wall. Though the pirate crew aroused quickly and returned fire, the King's ship continued the cannonade.

The fight was soon over and the pirate ship was lost! An acrid smell of gunpowder filled the air. Flames licked at the battered stairs to the top deck. Pirates beat at the flames, screaming obscenities, as though their fury could douse the fire.

Esme slunk low behind a barrel, her body trembling, her eyes black marbles, and her heart beating wildly. With a *whoosh,* the topsail burst into flames. Another cannonball exploded through the railing. Shrieks of pain mingled with the crack of shattered wood. Mangled pieces of the bulkhead lay in pools of blood. Fire raged across the deck. The captain's voice rang through the chaos. "We're lost. Throw over a lifeboat. All hands abandon ship."

Two pirates lowered a lifeboat and then dove from the railing, the first to reach its temporary safety.

"Get the fresh water barrel and I'll grab the moggie. We'll need her good luck or we're doomed." The captain shouted his final orders as he pulled Esme from behind a box.

Esme hurtled through the air, twisting and fighting the emptiness beneath her body. She was caught by eager hands and stuffed under the lifeboat seat. The scent of a damp rope beneath her feet mingled with the smell of sweat above her head. The First Mate leaped from the ship's rail and swam toward the lifeboat.

An explosion! Kegs of gunpowder crashed through the deck. The sails ignited. Shredded pieces of burning canvas flew upward, like flaming kites, and skittered through the air until they burned themselves out or drifted down, sizzling when they struck the water. Smoke and flames cast a gray and orange glow across the ocean. At last, the flaming mast of the pirate ship disappeared beneath a streak of oil and bubbles.

A chilling silence followed, where only a moment before the air was filled with shrieking chaos. A thick fog folded around the little boat, hiding it from the King's vengeance.

The First Mate whispered, "Quiet now, boys, and row like hell, because yer' lives depend upon it. For surely, we'll hang from the yardarm before nightfall, iffen' the King's men catch us."

For hours, the only sound was the splash of oars as the six surviving pirates rowed until the sweat poured from their bodies.

Safe beneath the First Mate's seat, the rhythm of the oars thumping the water matched the beat of Esme's heart. Her tail swayed gently from side to side as she slept. Later that day, the pirates were picked up by another ship.

She was safe at last, as the rescuers headed for a port on the coast of Maine where she would find shelter and the comfort of another crew.

In the years that followed, the sleek black cat with the short tail was highly sought after as the best ratter on the waterfront, but Esme never again let down her guard. Even as she slept, her tail would sway, as though ever watchful for her safety.

She eluded every effort to be taken aboard a vessel against her will, despite many enticements to join a particular ship. At the last moment, she would choose which ship to board, whether pirate or legal.

It was always one where the food was good, the men were kind, and there were just enough rats to keep her entertained on a long hot, dreary afternoon.

Black Cat's Legacy is available at Amazon ($3.99 e-book)
http://tinyurl.com/lrvevgm

Moonlight Madness

ix weeks after the World Trade Center attack on September 11, 2001, the nation continued to mourn.

Several days ago, the Sacramento Daily Sun editor burst into my office. "Clive. Pack your bags. You're going to Salem, Massachusetts, to cover their Halloween celebration. Let's give the subscribers something new to think about."

He had me at the words, 'pack your bags,' With yet another gut-wrenching editorial in my computer about the 341 firemen lost in the Towers, I was up for anything to get away from the 24/7 news cycle.

October 31st is big news in Salem. Every year. 250,000 visitors swarm the city to experience haunted houses, costume balls, live music, dances and holiday parades. This year, due to a full moon scheduled on October 31, 2001, the first full moon on that date since 1974, Salem planned even more spectacular events. The occurrence of a full moon on Halloween happens only four or five times each century. The next one isn't expected for another twenty years—October 31, 2020.

Entering Salem, I was impressed by the witches and goblins, pumpkins and ghouls decorating houses and businesses, much like we decorate for Christmas back home. Witches are big in Salem all year long, due to the history of the Salem witch trials, but this year, especially so, what with the full moon phenomenon. Apparently, Salem's city fathers thought the citizenry had grieved 9/11 long enough and should get their minds back onto business as usual. Let the nation grieve if it must. Salem would strike while the moon was full.

Cornstalks lined the streets. Jack-o-lanterns hung from each lamp post. Shopkeepers, decked out in witch and warlock, ghost and vampire costumes, hawked merchandise. Every shop window displayed witches and cauldrons, spirits and ghouls. Tourists clamored through the town atop horse drawn hay wagons and carts.

I ate lunch at a little diner and delighted in the attentions of a charming waitress with long black hair, shocking gold eyes and fluttering lashes. With a glance, Jenny churned up feelings I hardly remembered, being a widower well past middle-aged, and an almost regular church goer.

Imagine my surprise when she handed me a napkin with a message inside. *Meet me outside at 11:25 P.M. Come alone. I must see you.*

I left my lunch half-eaten and stumbled outside to ponder the situation. With her obvious charms, she had the pick of any young man; what could she possibly want with me? I interviewed shopkeepers and snapped photos of the holiday events that day and well into the evening. Even knowing it was a fool's errand, at 11:15 P.M, I was drawn back to the diner like a moth to a flame.

At 11:20 P.M. Jenny wiped down the last table, flipped over the *CLOSED* sign and locked the café door. She had nearly given up hope of finding a middle-aged man with silver-white hair and mustache. What were the odds that Clive should walk through the door at the last possible moment to change her destiny?

Jenny wrapped her cape around her shoulders and stepped out the front door. There Clive stood, as she had hoped. She was blessed with a sixth sense about the future, knowing when the phone would ring or a visitor would knock at her door. An oppressive spirit had even settled on her the morning of September 11, feeling something evil on the horizon. She had powers over men, but tonight, with the full moon overhead on this most auspicious date, her fate lay in the hands of this stranger. Without his cooperation, she could not escape the family curse.

"Hello. Thanks so much for coming." Jenny placed her small white hand on Clive's arm, hoping to bend his will to her needs. "You're the only one who can help me." She lifted her hand to dab at a tear.

"I'm happy to oblige. But, why do you ask for help from a stranger? Don't you have family or friends who could help you?"

Jenny lowered her head, brushing her lashes against her pale face. She allowed her lip to tremble as the tear trickled down her cheek. A white curl tumbled onto her forehead, seemingly out of place among her mass of black curls.

"Here, now, none of that." Clive brushed Jenny's hair back into place. "I'll help you if I can, my dear. Don't cry." He tipped up her chin and dried her tears with his handkerchief. "Now, give me a smile and tell me all about it."

"I fear you'll think me crazy, sir, but I swear I speak the truth." Jenny sat on a bench and began an inexplicable tale.

"I am a descendent of the judge who unjustly hanged Sarah Good as a witch in 1692, right here in Salem. Since Sarah Good's death, the judge's descendants have suffered a terrible curse. Upon the rare occasion, only about four or five times each century, when the full moon is overhead on All-Hollow's Eve, any female descendent between the age of 18 and 29 is in grave danger.

"As the full moon is upon us this night for the first time since 1974, and to avoid the curse, I must find a middle-aged man with long silver-white hair, who resembles the judge who sentenced my poor ancestor, Sarah, to death. Before midnight, a drop of this man's blood must voluntarily be placed on a particular stone that stands at the edge of town." Jenny's pale lips trembled most effectively. "Would you shed a drop of your blood on Sarah's commemorative stone to save me from the curse?"

"What kind of curse, my dear?" Clive raised a perplexed eyebrow.

"It is so terrible; I dare not speak it aloud." Whispering these words, Jenny clung to Clive's shoulder and wept piteously. Would it be enough to convince him to go with her to the stone? And, once there, could she muster the courage to do what must be done to stave off the curse?

Clive was speechless. Never had he encountered such a stunning creature that so captivated his heart within minutes of meeting. Never has such a ridiculous tale so captured his imagination. He was inclined to leap from the bench, take her by the hand and race to the stone in question. Only with great difficulty did he pummel his rash impulses into submission and sit back on the bench, staring up into the starry sky.

The full moon hung blood-red over the city, casting an orange glow across the sidewalks, still churning with costumed tourists, jostling and laughing, their joyous songs of nonsense carried into the black sky on the night breeze.

The young woman stirred in his arms, her sobs finally ceased. She dashed tears from her cheeks and looked up at him. "You will help me, won't you? I'm so desperate. I only need a teeny-weeny drop of blood, really. I'd be ever so grateful."

If she truly believed her outrageous tale, considering the unusual request, even a gentleman couldn't help wondering, *how grateful*? On the other hand, just exactly how much was a *teeny-weeny* drop of blood and just how crazy was this charming girl?

Clive shivered. The breeze rustled the corn husks tied to the lamp posts. A thin cloud crept across the center of the moon, seeming to cut it in half.

Clive glanced at his watch. *11:40 P.M.* "Well, let's get on with it. Can we walk to the stone?" He would humor her and see where all this would lead. His hand rested around a small penknife in his pocket. *If a tiny drop of blood is all it takes to satisfy her fantasy and win her gratitude, I can do that.*

The wind picked up and whistled overhead as the cemetery loomed into view. Groups of tourists ambled among the grave stones. Raucous laughter burst from the direction of Bridget Bishop and Martha Corey's graves, also victims of the 1692 Salem witch trials. One would think it was an amusement park rather than a cemetery from the sounds of merriment coming from the shadows.

Jenny squealed when a man dressed as a vampire loomed from the bushes.

Clive put his arm around her shoulder and pulled her close. She was really a dear little thing, and his heart stirred. He wanted so to calm her fears. Perhaps he'd bring her coffee in bed tomorrow morning...

Sarah Good's commemorative stone gleamed in the moonlight.

Jenny ran her fingers over the grooves in the stone forming the letters– *Sarah Good 1653 – 1692.* "Poor thing. I'm so sorry, Sarah. Please forgive my ancestor." Jenny glanced at her watch. "Are you ready?" She drew a huge serrated bread knife from her purse. "We don't have much time. I only have two more minutes. Clive?" Jenny's beautiful smile, only moments ago holding so much promise, faded, replaced by a fiendish leer. Only his blood splashed across the accursed stone would make her smile now.

At the sight of Jenny's wild eyes gleaming in the moonlight, Clive stepped back. The thrill of the lovely lady and moonlight adventure faded and common sense finally prevailed. Jenny had no intention of settling for a pricked finger and a *drop* of blood.

With the knife in her hand, she crept closer and closer with murder in her eye.

"Hold on, there, young lady." He backed away, glancing left and right. Where had all the costumed tourists gone? The witches and ghosts and even the vampire had disappeared at the first sight of Jenny's knife.

In the distance, the town clock began to strike. Twelve o'clock... the witching hour. *Bong...bong...bong.* The hour that a real witch, if there was such a thing, might easily murder a stranger to satisfy her twisted notion of an imaginary family curse.

Bong...bong...bong. Clive's dull life suddenly held a great deal more appeal. How he wished he was back in New York and had never heard of Salem. *Bong...bong...bong.*

Bong...bong... Jenny shrieked and rushed at him, the knife raised...

Paralyzed with fear, Clive threw up his hands, closed his eyes and held his breath, waiting for the death blow. *Bong.* Midnight!

Seconds ticked by. Clive ran his hands up and down his chest. "I'm still alive?" He opened his eyes.

Jenny's cape and the bread knife lay on the ground, but... Where was Jenny? Had she waited seconds too long to strike and the curse taken her? But where? How?

Sarah Good's gravestone gleamed in the moonlight. A small black cat hunched beside the stone, her tail whipping around her black toes. A white blaze crept over her nose, across one golden eye, ending beside her ear. She stared up at Clive, terror in those golden eyes, such as to soften the hardest heart. *Meow?*

"Jenny?" Clive walked closer to the stone. Wasn't there a fable about witches turning into black cats? He'd never believed such tales before, but... He stroked the little cat and peered into her eyes. "Jenny?" He gasped. Jenny's golden eyes stared back. The curse. It was true. "She needed me to protect her from the curse. She still needs me."

He would write his 2000 words newspaper story about Salem, about the haunted houses and the costume ball and the decorations and the Halloween parades. The story would be colorful and for a few minutes the Sacramento Daily Sun readers could forget the tragedy that took almost 3000 lives on September 11, 2001.

He would write about tonight being the first full moon on Halloween for the last twenty-seven years, but, he would not write about a 300-year-old curse that turned a Salem witch into a little black cat. Who would believe it?

Clive cradled Jenny in his arms as he walked back to town. "Don't worry, Jenny. I'll take care of you. You don't have to worry about anything ever again."

The Halloween Bag

om closed the door and skipped down the sidewalk to his '57 souped-up T-bird.

Penny's shrieks followed him down the sidewalk, but he didn't care. He always took what he wanted from women until they grew tiresome, and then he'd toss them away. Women were like shoes. When the shine was gone, you got a new pair.

Penny was harder to leave than some of the others, but what point to stick around? Women always expected commitment and Penny was no exception. Tom wasn't the committing type.

Tom checked his rear-view mirror and ran his hands through his carrot-red hair. Not to worry. He'd have another girlfriend, probably within the week. He stomped the gas and sped away.

Penny clutched her black cat to her breast, "I should never have allowed myself to get involved. I thought Tom was different." A brown Maltese cat, a golden-eyed, pure white cat and a tan blue-eyed beauty from Oriental ancestry, hunkered nearby, commiserating with her sorrow.

Penny twisted her wineglass. Reflections from the glass cast a rainbow across the far wall. Penny took a sip and lifted her head. "Lord knows, an orange one won't make me feel any better." A faint smile twitched her lips. "Perhaps, though, I should give it more thought."

She patted the black longhaired cat in her lap. He gazed up at her and yawned.

"Come on, guys, let's get a snack. Then, I'm going shopping." Her feline menagerie followed her to the kitchen. Penny gazed at the four, squatted around a pile of Friskies like the four spokes of a wheel; black, brown, white and tan. "Yes, I think an orange one is exactly what I need," Penny whispered.

With a few phone calls, Penny learned that Tom had a lunch meeting at a little restaurant on Main Street. She smiled and nodded, "Let the games begin."

Penny pulled a dusty box from the top shelf in the garage. She raised the lid and removed a black hat sporting a long red feather. She ran her fingers over its velvety texture, from nib to tip. "This will do nicely." A mist of dust rose from the feather and disappeared in a wisp of breeze.

She pawed through her closet until she found, tucked between a tweed suit from the 1980's and a much older leather jacket, a black pantsuit with shoulder pads and bellbottom pants. She shook the wrinkles from the jacket and frowned at the tiny moth hole in the left sleeve.

Has it been that long since I used this outfit? I could have sworn it was just a couple of years ago. A chuckle of delight bubbled in her throat.

Donning the black pantsuit and the red feathered hat, she added a bangle bracelet and a pair of gold hoop earrings to the ensemble and nodded in satisfaction at the image reflected in her hall mirror.

Penny drove downtown and parked a half block from Marvelous Marvin's Magic Shop, next door to the restaurant where Tom was meeting a friend.

She stood outside the magic shop, as though admiring the items in the window. In less time than it takes to tell, Tom strode down the street, his bright red hair blowing in the wind. She turned toward him, caught his eye, and then dashed into the magic shop. Once inside the store, an elaborate sound system emitted shrieks and squeals of organ music, eerie enough to chill one's very soul.

Tom followed her into the store….as she knew he would. "Penny, is that you?"

Penny did not answer, but hurried through the darkened aisles toward a dimly lit corner piled high with boxes, capes, and baskets heaped with assorted magic tricks and magician's paraphernalia.

Tom followed…as she knew he would, until they were in the furthest dark corner, where the black light overhead caused the Magic Marvin's Magic Shop logo on a stack of black shopping bags to glow in a neon aura.

She turned to face him. The feather in her hat gently waved, caressed by the breeze from the air conditioner.

Tom's gaze followed the drifting red feather…as she knew he would. "Penny? What are you doing here? Are you going to a costume party?" His gaze remained locked on the swaying feather.

"No, I was waiting for you."

"For me? Don't be tiresome. I told you… We have nothing more to talk about."

"Oh, but I think we do." She tapped her long red fingernail three times on the pile of black Marvelous Marvin's shopping bags and whispered, "Dinkle, Dinkle, Catzenwinkle."

Tom disappeared. The top shopping bag now displayed the image of a vivid orange striped cat with round glowing eyes, staring wildly from its paper prison.

Penny carried the bag to the counter. "I'll take this one." She paid for the bag and left the store.

Back in her apartment, Penny poured another glass of wine, filled a plate with crackers and cheese and summoned her feline friends.

They came from under the table, from the top of the sofa, from under the bed, down off the fireplace, stretching and yawning. Like four spokes of a wheel, black, brown, white and tan, they circled the shopping bag decorated with the vivid face of an orange cat with glowing eyes. Penny tossed each cat a bite of cheese.

She nibbled a cracker, sipped her wine and set her glass on the counter. She grasped the shopping bag and tipped it upside down, "This is Tom," she said.

A carrot-orange striped cat spilled onto the floor. He gazed wildly around the room, his big round eyes filled with terror...confusion written on his face.

The four cats nibbled their cheese and watched the newcomer with some amusement.

"Welcome your new changeling companion. Just like the rest of you, Tom has come to live with us." Penny tossed Tom a bite of cheese. She folded the black shopping bag and shoved it into the wastebasket.

Halloween and the Leger Hotel

O ne Halloween weekend, our human mother took me and Sissy to the Leger Hotel in Mokelume Hills in the Sierra Mountains. She left us in the room while she went downstairs to look around the hotel.

Being a couple of curious cats, we squeezed through the slightly open full-length glass windows onto the balcony. According to the brochure on the nightstand, that's where the prostitutes used to sit, advertising their wares, back in the gold rush days of the late1800's. Oh my.

A noise drew us back inside. Imagine our surprise to see the wispy outline of an old guy with whiskers sitting on the sofa. "Excuse me. Every year on Halloween, I get the chanct' to ask for help to move on to the *here-after.* Can you help me?"

The hair on my neck stood on end and my tail puffed up twice its size. (That happens when a cat gets startled.) "You're a ghost. What can we do?"

Sissy's eyes were the size of half-dollars. *Hissstt.*

"Name's Joe Harrigan. Me and my partner had a gold mine nearby back in 1876. My partner accidently shot hisself, but he writ out his will before he died, leavin' everthing to me.

"I come to town thinkin' to aggrieve his death with a bottle. I hid George's will in the back panel of the armoire, there in the corner, 'afore I went down to the bar. The sheriff *calcumlated* that I kilt' George to steal his gold. Bein' skunk-drunk, I plumb forgot to mention the will in the armoire, so they adjudged me guilty and hanged me dead right outside that there windda'." Old George waved toward the balcony.

"Oncet' dead, my head sorta' cleared and I remembered the will, but 'acourse it was too late. I shoulda' gone on to the *here-after*, but trouble is, Hell wouldn't have me because I was innocent a murder, you see. But bein' convicted of a murder all official-like in a *court a' law*, Heaven wouldn't have me neither. I've been 'ahoverin' *in-between* ever since, hopin' someone would find that air' will and clear my good name. It's doubtful I deserve Heaven but I'd like a crack at it."

"How come you don't ask a *person* to help?" I twitched a skeptical ear.

"Every year on Halloween when I get a chance to ask for help, folks runs off yellin', 'I seen a ghost,' and ask for another room. Sometimes they got a dog, but dogs growl and hide under the bed."

Sissy and I exchanged glances. She nodded. "It's true—dogs are stupid."

The old guy's aura faded. "Look, girls, I'm about at the end of my rope...no pun intended. If I don't *move on* to my final reward pretty quick, I could be stuck here forever. Will you help me get the will out of the armoire?"

I nodded. "Let's do it." How could we deny a fellow the chance for a crack at Heaven? We scratched at the armoire door until it opened and Sissy clawed at the back panel.

"That's it. Give it all ya' got." Joe's aura hovered overhead. "It sorta slides in when you push on it. There. See that paper stickin' out? Pull it out." Sissy sunk her teeth into the corner of the paper and eased it through the crack.

"Hurry. You did it." Old Joe crowed. "I'm saved. Now, if you'll show it to the authorities, maybe they'll clear my good name, at last and I can move on."

Mom came back to the room and saw us pawing the paper. "What have you girls got?" She picked up the faded will and read it. "Where did this come from?"

Joe's aura drifted out through the open window, his whiskered face cracked in a grin.

Mom carried us downstairs to the manager's office. "My cats found this up in Room Two. It looks like a holographic will. Your Historic Society might want to take a look at it."

"Room Two?" The manager took the paper. "I've heard complaints of that room being haunted. What have you got?" He read the paper...

Joe didn't shoot me. I done it akleenin' my gun. I got no fambly and Joe Harrigan gets my share a the mine. October 30, 1876 George Harris

The manager pointed toward the stuffed effigy of a body hanging on the balcony. "Well, I'll be. They hanged Joe Harrigan from that very spot. This could clear his name. He's buried up on Boot Hill. You folks should go up and see his grave."

Dad drove us to the cemetery and found Old Joe's tombstone. *Joe Harrigan—Born 1818—Hanged October 31, 1876.*

Sissy said, "Do you suppose Old Joe made it through the pearly gates, after all?"

I twitched a whisker "I think St. Peter gave Old Joe a fair trial when he got there," I said. "He sure never got justice back in 1876 in Mokelume Hills when he was hanged by mistake."

Here, Kitten, Kitten

They were feral cats, living on location at my work site. Every few days, my daughter and I fed the pregnant tortoiseshell cat. The weeks passed and she came to our call, knowing we would feed her. In time, the kittens were born, evidenced by mama cat's profile. Each day we thought, "Today we will see them," but days passed without a baby in sight. We thought the kittens had died.

One day, we saw the three little waifs—one female kitten, the image of her mother, a rose-colored kitten, and the black male with one eye completely closed by infection.

We filled a cardboard box with towels, and I crawled under the bushes. "Here kitten, kitten," and the rose-colored kitten came to me. I popped her into the box and crawled further, trying to catch the other two. "Here, kitten, kitten."

How I wished they could know how their lives would change if they came to me. Toys, good food, immunizations, no fleas, and a warm bed.

"Here, kitten, kitten," and I held the tortoiseshell kit by the scruff of her neck. The box trembled with their mewing and scratching. Their cries inspired me to go back for the black brother. I crawled further into the bushes and reached for him. My fingers barely touched his soft fur, but he scampered away. My lunch hour was nearly over and I had to leave him behind.

Several months passed and the rose-colored kitten and her sister became fixtures in my house, frolicking up and down the kitty-pole, napping across my lap, kicking and fighting mock battles, and attacking catnip mice with a vengeance. With full tummies, they curled together on a fluffy bed at night.

"Here kitten, kitten." The sisters hear my call and run to me. They reach up my leg, purr and rub their little heads into my hands, begging to be picked up. They don't remember the day I left their brother behind, but I do, and it hurts me to think of him, perhaps hungry, perhaps sick, never knowing the joy of a human touch.

You might say, "It's not his fault. The black kitten can't know how dramatically his life could change. He would surrender if he had the capacity to understand. He's afraid and he's doing what comes naturally. He's just a kitten."

He's still there, they tell me, those who catch a glimpse of him from time to time. He's a grown feral cat now, one of the untouchables that scoot into the bushes, frightened by the sound of a human step.

And so I return to the bushes from time to time. "Here, kitten, kitten," One day, I hope he will respond and allow me to give him a better life.

There is so much suffering in the world. I think of all the sick bodies I have no means to heal, the hungry mouths I cannot feed, the people around the world who live daily under the threat of death for their religious beliefs.

I cannot change the suffering of the world, but this little cat's life is something I should have the power to change. He has a body I am able to heal, a mouth I can feed. My heart aches that I'm unable to do even this simple thing...

And so from time to time, I return, crawl under the bushes and call, "Here kitten, kitten. Please, Lord, let me change just one small injustice in this world. Here, kitten, kitten. Please come to me."

Kilcuddy Kitty

ilcuddy Kitty stretched out in the sunny butcher shop window, anxiously awaiting Shamus O'Reilly. Any minute now, he'd arrive to open the shop. The sun's first rays lit up the posters in the window.

Beef Kidneys—$.39 a pound,
Oxtails—$.15 a pound,
Beef bones—$.10 a pound.

Since the attack on Pearl Harbor last December, housewives accepted the scarcity of meat available at the butcher shop, knowing that the best cuts were sent to the troops. Dealing with the restrictions of rationing without complaint was considered patriotic.

Kilcuddy Kitty rolled over in the sun, recalling last night's events after Shamus flicked out the lights and locked the doors. Kilcuddy had settled to nap atop the roll of butcher paper behind the meat counter. Shattering glass in the back room roused him from slumber. He leaped to the top of the counter. Hunkered down, ears pricked and muscles taunt, he riveted his gaze toward the doorway.

Footsteps crunched through broken glass! Fear smell emanated from a masked figure entering the shop. A stream of light from a flashlight played across the glass counter toward the cash register.

Kilcuddy's hair stood on end. The tip of his tail flipped from side to side.

The thief moved closer.

With a mighty leap, Kilcuddy Kitty landed on the intruder's shoulders. *Yoww!!*

The thief shrieked, jerked from left to right, trying to dislodge the claws digging into his back. In his frenzy, his torchlight fell to the floor.

Warm blood filled Kilcuddy's mouth as he sank his fangs into the man's neck.

The prowler cursed, grabbed Kilcuddy by the back of his neck and flung him across the room.

Thump! Kilcuddy landed in a heap. Dazed, he heard frantic mumbling and scuttling as the intruder plunged through the darkness and escaped out the back window. The thud of his footsteps pounded down the alley and then faded away.

Kilcuddy lay on the floor, his ears ringing, head aching, tasting the man's blood in his mouth. *Odd, human blood tastes different than chicken blood. Sweeter, somehow.* Or, was it the satisfaction of stopping a burglar and protecting Shamus's shop that tasted so sweet? Without a doubt, he had foiled the thief's attempt to rob the store and steal the best cuts of meat...

Pushing last night's memories from his mind, Kilcuddy Kitty rolled over and presented his tummy to the warm morning sunshine. Shamus would soon be here. What fine beef trimmings or snippets of kidneys would he spoon into Kilcuddy's bowl as a reward for thwarting the burglar? Do cats ever receive medals for bravery? Perhaps they'd host a parade. He'd be Grand Marshall and sit beside the mayor's pretty wife.

The click of a key in the back room. Shamus O'Reilly had arrived at last. "Begorra, the window is shattered and me clean floor is covered with glass." The shop owner rushed to the cash register and punched the proper keys. The drawer popped open, revealing neat rows of cash from yesterday's sales. "Sure and the saints have blessed me. Me money is still here!"

Seeing nothing else amiss, Shamus swept up the broken glass in the storeroom, mumbling such words as cannot be repeated in a *G-rated* storybook.

Kilcuddy Kitty cruised against the cash register, his whiskers a-tingle, his back arched in sheer anticipation, as he patiently waited for Shamus to return from the back room and lavish him with the praise and treats he so richly deserved.

His mouth watered. Would his reward be a whopping $.62 a pound salmon steak, such as the mayor's wife bought each Friday afternoon? Didn't Shamus always hold back the best cuts for her? Though, where she got all the ration coupons for such a purchase was enough to give one pause... Other housewives rarely had enough money or meat coupons for such culinary delights.

At last, Shamus stalked into the shop, shaking his broom. "So, there you are, Kilcuddy Kitty, standing about as usual, while I clean up the mess. Like as not you slept right through the scoundrel breaking me fine window. What luck he didn't come into the shop and steal me hard-earned cash. You're a poor store minder, you worthless cat. Me thinks I should get rid of you and get a good watchdog!"

What? What? The unfairness of it! Kilcuddy Kitty arched his back and hissed. *The ingratitude. After all I've done!* His tail puffed up like a bristle brush. He sprang off the meat counter. How unjust the master. How unmerited the disparagement. Hadn't he warded off the perpetrator, risked life and limb to save Shamus's cash, and suffered a *bonk* on the noggin when he was so unceremoniously pitched against the wall? Where was his praise, his medal and parade? Where even the scrap of meat in his bowl? *Oh, deliver me from the injustice of man.*

Shamus stood with his broom in his hand as Kilcuddy Kitty dashed into the storeroom, leaped through the broken window and bounded down the back alley, howling. *And fare thee well, Shamus O'Reilly, for I'll never darken your doorstep again.*

Kilcuddy never forgave old Shamus or returned to the butcher shop.

Every Saturday night, you'll find Shamus at Sean O'Flanahan's pub, whining to any who will listen. "Alas, later that day, I found a flashlight on the floor and blood on the cash register. Me good cat, Kilcuddy Kitty, must have run the bugger off before he could steal me money. And, now because of my sins, I've lost me best pal."

Whereupon, Shamus weeps and orders another beer. Soon his drinking buddies tire of his whining and turn their backs on him.

And what, might you wonder, happened to Kilcuddy Kitty? Folks say he took up with the mayor's pretty wife. When asked if he'll ever forgive Shamus and return to the butcher shop, Kilcuddy Kitty winks and says. "Why should I? Life is grand with the mayor's wife. Every Friday she goes to Shamus O'Reilly's butcher shop with another ration book and buys the best cuts of meat. I love the salmon, but some have asked. 'How does she come by so many ration coupons?'

"I think there's something fishy going on…"

Kitty's Blessing

nce, in a faraway land, on a crisp winter afternoon, Miss Kitty strode across a hillside, a contented pussy cat, her tummy full and her breath pungent with the after-taste of this morning's breakfast mouse. She settled on a warm rock for a snooze in the sunshine near a flock of sheep tended by a group of shepherds. The flock moved down the hillside. With her tail curled around her nose, Miss Kitty fell asleep as the bleating of lambs faded into the distance.

Interrupted from her catnap by the twittering of a bird, Miss Kitty's eye peeked open. *What's this?* The tip of her tail drifted from side to side. She slipped off the rock and inched toward the unsuspecting after-breakfast snack. Miss Kitty's whiskers snapped to attention. Every hair on her head stood upright. She was a silent warrior armed with experience, girded with strength, clad with skill. The bird was within striking range; distance calculated (ten feet, six and a half inches); wind velocity (twenty-one and a half mph from the south-southeast); thrust computed; muscles poised. She leaped.

The striped instrument of death hurtled toward the beautiful white bird. At the last moment, she fluttered off the bush. Miss Kitty seized her wing and pulled her to the ground.

The white bird shrieked. "Wait! Don't eat me. I'll make it worth your while if you spare my life."

Much impressed by the bird's bravery, as misguided as it was under the circumstances, Miss Kitty paused, curiosity being a trait of her breed, often misquoted as being the method of her kind's demise. "What can possibly change my mind, my pretty?" Holding the bird's wing firmly with one paw, she tilted her left ear and licked her lips.

The white bird lifted her elegant head and folded her free wing against her quivering body. "If you set me free, I promise, ere the night is over, you will receive a great blessing that will bring honor to you and all your descendants."

Kitty loosened her grip slightly to ponder the bird's message. If true, a *blessing* would be a fine legacy to leave her descendants. Much more likely, the blessing was just a ploy to escape. But, what did she have to lose? Intrigued, and frankly, still burping this morning's mouse, she agreed. "I'll let you go this time, but if you're fooling me, next time we meet, I'll show no mercy." She lifted her paw.

The grateful captive fluttered from her grasp. She circled, dipping low over Miss Kitty's head. "I've told the truth. Ere the night is over. I promise," she cried and disappeared behind a puffy white cloud.

"A blessing, indeed. *Humph!*" Miss Kitty shook her body from nose to tail, dispelling the notion that she had swallowed the lie and foolishly believed such a story.

As the full moon rose and the stars blinked across the night sky, Miss Kitty returned to town. *Now, where shall I sleep tonight?* She came upon a cave where cows and a donkey nodded, warming the grotto with their breath. In the corner, a lamb lay curled next to its mother.

This will do nicely. Miss Kitty jumped into the box of straw near the cow, turned around three times, and then curled her body into a ball. Gentle snuffles from the lamb, combined with the cows' warm breath, created the perfect atmosphere for a long winter nap. Miss Kitty was soon fast asleep and dreaming. *Dots of white sheep ambled down the dark hillside. Overhead, the white bird darted across a yellow moon as shepherds moved their flock toward town.*

As a pair of gentle hands lifted Kitty from the straw, she opened her eyes.

The young bearded man set her gently on the ground. "Here, kitty, won't you give up your warm bed? It's just the right size for the Baby." He laid the swaddled infant in the straw where Kitty's body had molded and warmed a circle of straw just the size to fit the new-born infant.

Who is this child that stirs my heart with the faintest glimpse of his precious face? Miss Kitty lay down beneath the manger, curled her toes into a semi-circle, amazed and fascinated by the unexpected events in the stable.

The father brought the mother water and then tenderly covered her with his cloak.

Shepherds from the hillside entered the stable and knelt at the feet of the Babe.

Two white birds fluttered through the open door, circled and settled on the edge of the manger. Surely, one was the same bird she had freed that afternoon. Wonder of wonders, a brilliant light shone above the manger. Where the birds had come to rest, now angels hovered on each side of the Baby.

When the visitors had gone, in the stillness of the stable the family slept while the angels kept watch.

Miss Kitty approached and addressed the angel she recognized from earlier in the day. "Angel, I know this is the Promised One the world has long awaited. The others brought gifts. I feel unworthy. I have no gift to give."

"Tonight, without complaint, you gave up your warm bed for the Christ Child. In return you received a great blessing that you and your descendants can treasure for generations to come. Miss Kitty, the Christ Child wants only the gift of our love and obedience."

Miss Kitty curled her tail around her nose and began to dream of naps in the sunshine, chasing mice, catching birds—perhaps she would forgo that pleasure in the future. One never knows when the bird might be an angel—or when a good deed might turn into a blessing, but none like the blessing she had just received–the chance to warm the Christ Child's bed.

48

Sitka's Story

Sitka's story is an excerpt from my cozy cat mystery novel, **Black Cat and the Lethal Lawyer***. It takes place in Texas near the Mexican border. While confusion and chaos abound at the ranch, Sitka, the mountain lion, raises her two cubs out on the prairie.*

ar from the ranch house in the mountains to the east, Sitka, the mountain lion, lounged on a rocky overhang, watching her two cubs tumble and wrestle on the warm rocks below.

Their bright little eyes danced in new discovery as birds flew past the den and dragonflies flitted near the overhang. Their ears perked at every sound. A hawk flying overhead—the snap of a bush where a small animal ventured—the wind rustling in the bushes below the den.

At a sudden noise, Sitka's head swung to the left. The kittens stood rigidly at attention when the distant sound of a rumbling truck reached their ears, caught in the shifting wind blowing through the canyon below.

Sitka scanned the canyon wall and half-raised her body from the rock, alert and searching for anything that might threaten her family.

Sensing their mother's distress, the kittens raced back into the den and huddled together. Four little blue eyes nestled in a mass of spotted gold fur peered through the darkness.

Sitka strained to listen. The rumble of the truck grew fainter and then stopped. She vocalized a soft chirp and began to purr. The perceived danger had passed and the cubs were safe to resume their play. The cautious kittens crept slowly into the bright sunshine.

Within minutes, Sitka resumed her position near the front of the rock, lazily switching her tail as the cubs wrestled in mock battle once more.

The male cub, spying a new game, left his sister on the rock and jumped at his mother's tail, batting it from side to side, perhaps imagining it to be some sort of elusive beast.

Toward evening, Sitka crouched on an overhanging rock formation on the southern canyon wall. Nearby, a white-tailed deer unsuspectingly paused to graze on an outcropping of dry grass. Sitka had stalked the deer, waiting for the exact moment for it to be within striking distance.

Silvery-gray fur on the lion's head blended into lighter patches around her jaws and glistened in the afternoon sun. All ninety pounds of her feline body tensed, ready to leap. She flexed her claws, gathered her legs beneath her powerful body and sprinted the last twenty feet across the rock, leaping onto the deer's back. With one powerful chomp, she broke its neck and bore it to the ground. Sitka seized her kill by the throat and dragged it to a nearby pile of shrubs where she fed on the meat. She then scratched grass and brush over the body to camouflage it from other predators. Over the next two or three days, she would return often to feed until she had eaten the whole carcass. Within weeks, Sitka would lead the cubs to her kill to begin to feed on meat, but today, the cubs were completely dependent on their mother's milk.

In the nearby rocky alcove, the three month old cubs peered across the plains, watching anxiously for their mother's return. The alcove provided a measure of protection from the hot sun and chilly nights. Instinctively, they knew not to leave its safety. Growing bored with waiting, they curled in the den to sleep.

The kits were startled from sleep when Sitka jumped onto the rock. She lay down, sleepy and her hunger satiated. She groomed the kittens, tumbling them vigorously around the enclosure.

They kneaded gently on her tawny belly to hasten the life sustaining milk.

Sitka closed her golden eyes and nodded. A slight noise in the distance brought her to wakefulness. She scanned the plains but nothing moved within her view. All was silent, except for the cry of a hawk flying high overhead and the chirp of the cicadas in the rocks. She closed her eyes and slept.

Black Cat and the Lethal Lawyer is available at Amazon in e-book and paperback
http://tinyurl.com/q3qrgyu

Only in America

I was born on a cool spring morning under a woodpile in the country, a fair distance from the nearest vestiges of the big city. My mother taught me all she knew, and I often fell asleep, listening to the sound of her purring and the thrum of her heartbeat. She shared all the secrets of the universe, which are known to all cats.

She taught me patience through the art of field mouse stalking. She taught me hygiene by learning the importance of washing behind one's ears. I learned communication skills and the art of listening when my attention strayed from mother's lessons and she cuffed my ears. I shall never forget those carefree kitten days, for they were filled with peace and joy and love.

I filled the afternoon with long naps in the sunshine and grooming my sleek black body, carefully licking each white foot until my body glistened.

Mother and I spent many happy days basking in the meadow, until the dreadful day the dogcatcher drove by and caught sight of us sleeping on the woodpile. I suppose he found us a blight on the neighborhood with no humans to care for us.

Mother escaped, but before I knew what happened, he cornered me and tossed me into a truck. I heard mother crying as the truck drove away, down the road toward… What? I have come to believe it was destiny.

We arrived at our destination, the city POUND, where the smell of dogs and cats filled the room. I was put into a small cage with a box of sand in the corner, surrounded by the pitiful cries of cats and kittens. In the next room, I heard the horrendous din of dog sounds. People carried cats back and forth. Sometimes they never came back. At night the older cats whispered, saying that many of the cats were *put to sleep*, which didn't sound so bad, but the way they said it made me wonder. They also mentioned *adoption* and though that sounded worse than *put to sleep*, they spoke of it as a more desirable circumstance. I hoped that one day I might experience *adoption*, if it meant escaping from kitty prison.

On the sixth day of captivity, a man, a lady and a child came into the room where my jail cell was located and removed me from the cage. The stroke of their hands was frightening, but after a bit, I rather liked it. Eventually, I was carried from the room, stuck with a needle and put into a small box. My box jiggled and jounced and the sound of a vehicle again roared in my ears. If this was *adoption*, it wasn't so great after all, as I thought it a very real possibility that the end of life was near.

Imagine my surprise when I was released from the box into a large lovely house with a number of people running hither and yon. Before long, I became accustomed to the goings-on in the house and figured out the people were obviously here to fulfill my every wish.

My favorite napping place late in the afternoon was on the dining room table in a spot of sunshine. Just about the time I would settle down on the white linen tablecloth between the plates and glasses, the maid would shriek and shoo me onto the floor.

As time went on, I lost my fear of the man and we became great friends. Many times he would take me into his office and put me in his lap in his rocking chair. As we rocked, he would talk to himself and stroke my head. I could not understand his words but sensed his distress from the tone of his voice. I purred and gazed into his eyes to convey my concern for his problems. He seemed to take great comfort from this and shortly, would leave me in the chair, smiling and nodding his head as though we had solved his problem. Thus, I knew my counsel was good.

I recall a day when my man put me in the traveling box and

returned me to the pound. I regretted sleeping on the dining room table and supposed it had to do with that. After a night in the cage, a man took me to a small white room gleaming with chrome. The room began to spin when he stuck my leg with a needle.

I awoke feeling dreadful. Everything hurt and I chucked up my dinner. I felt pretty bad for a couple of days, but I was much improved by the time the child returned from camp. I never understood just what happened. Perhaps it was the flu, or something I ate.

As time passed, I was surprised to learn that my man was very important, as men go. As busy as the house had been, it became even busier. We moved to Washington into a big white house and my man and I now rocked in his chair in an oval room with a red phone. Now as I understand it, my man had become the most important *Man* in the country and my lady is called the First Lady. I suppose the child is the First Child.

Apparently I have become pretty popular too. People with cameras get excited when I walk into the room and say, "Here comes Sox!" They make a fuss over me and everyone rushes to take my picture.

As I look back over my life, I get goose bumps thinking about the great country we live in. Only in America could a cat born in a woodpile end up in Washington. Only in America, could a fellow be snatched from obscurity and have the opportunity to make something of himself. And only in America, could a cat from humble beginnings find himself in the most important seat in the nation, literally in a rocking chair, in the Oval Office, in the White House, counselor to the President of the United States, Bill Clinton.

I think from now on, people should call me First Cat.

Clyde's Funeral

*This is an excerpt from my novel, **Mrs. Odboddy – Hometown Patriot**. Mrs. Odboddy's neighbor, Clyde, fell off the roof trying to rescue Mrs. Turnbull's cat, Mitzi. The cat survived the fall. Clyde didn't. We join his friends and relatives at his funeral.*

Agnes followed her granddaughter, Katherine, into the funeral parlor and gazed around the chapel.

There was Clyde's daughter, weeping in the front row. She hadn't been seen in Newbury for over ten years. Wasn't it a shame how children live three states away, never visit their parents until they lay dead in their casket, and then weep their heart out on the front row of the funeral parlor? Maybe they were more tears of shame than tears of love and loss.

Obviously still feeling responsible for Clyde's death, Mrs. Turnbull wept alongside Clyde's daughter. What was in that box at her feet? *Surely, it's not her cat, Mitzie!* The corner of the lid lifted, revealing a pink nose and a black ear. By golly, it was. Guess Mrs. Turnbull figured since Clyde died trying to save Mitzie's life, she should pay her respects at his funeral.

Pastor Lickleiter's wife sat in the back row, though it was doubtful Clyde had ever darkened the door of the First Church of the Evening Star and Everlasting Light. Apparently it was the duty of the pastor's wife to attend every service her husband conducted, be it christening, wedding or funeral. Mrs. Lickleiter had no sense of fashion, but she was a good pastor's wife, if nothing else.

Several other neighbors made up the remainder of the guests, along with Mrs. Roosevelt, her body guard and her secretary, Tommy. Mrs. Roosevelt and Tommy sat across the aisle from Clyde's daughter.

Pastor Lickleiter began the service with a prayer and mentioned Clyde's good points. They were few. And, his achievements in life; they were fewer.

The pastor spent the majority of his talk, describing the finer points of Clyde's final attempt to save Mrs. Turnbull's cat. All eyes turned toward the box jiggling at Mrs. Turnbull's feet.

At the mention of the Mitzie, Clyde's daughter broke out in a fresh display of wailing.

Mrs. Turnbull wailed even louder, nearly drowning out Clyde's daughter's heaving sobs.

Pastor Lickleiter paused, giving the ladies time to compose themselves. After several sniffles and a good deal of nose blowing, he continued.

Some twelve minutes later, Pastor Lickleiter concluded his final prayer. "Now, I'll invite any who wish to share your remembrances of Clyde, please come forward now."

Mrs. Roosevelt stood and walked to the pulpit. She looked very comfortable at the podium, as she'd had plenty of practice over the past year, going from one fundraiser to another and heading multiple political and charitable events.

"Clyde and I were great friends when I lived in the Hudson River Valley during my preteen years. Clyde was a distant cousin on my mother's side. But, during those impressionable years, he was more than a friend.

"Clyde was lots of fun, and he was a great animal lover. He had a little black and white spotted dog that followed us everywhere. When we grew older, I lost track of Clyde, but from what I remember about him, I'm not surprised that Clyde risked his life, trying to save Mitzie."

Meow!

As Mitzie responded to her name, all heads again swiveled to the box at Mrs. Turnbull's feet and Mrs. Turnbull burst into a fresh frenzy of weeping. She leaned down, unsnapped the lid and pulled Mitzie into her lap. Mitzie wiggled and then settled with another plaintive *Mew!*

Mrs. Roosevelt paused, and then spoke again. "Farewell, dear Clyde, until we meet again." She stepped out from the podium and returned to her seat.

The silence in the room was palpable. Most of the guests dabbed their eyes, whether they had ever given old Clyde much thought before or not, because in death, Mrs. Roosevelt made him more lovable than he had ever been in life and to a man, they grieved the fact that they had never given him more than a passing 'howdy.'

Pastor Lickleiter invited others to speak, but who could follow Mrs. Roosevelt after the speech she made? There were no takers, not even his daughter or Mrs. Turnbull.

"Then I'll invite you all to stand," instructed Pastor Lickleiter, "and come forward if you wish to extend your final farewell to our dear friend, followed by luncheon in the next room."

While many of the crowd headed out the door and into the dining room, Mrs. Turnbull jumped from her seat with Mitzie cradled in her arms. She moved into the line behind Clyde's daughter and her husband. They paused beside the casket, glanced at Clyde and moved back to the front row.

Mrs. Turnbull stepped up to the casket, wailing, with Mitzie clutched to her breast. She leaned over the casket. Tears dripped from her cheeks onto his faded lapel. Then, she held Mitzie up until her furry front feet hovered over the edge of the casket.

What was she doing? Allowing Mitzie to pay her last respect? Agnes gasped as Mrs. Turnbull lowered the cat into the casket. *Oh, my Stars!*

Whatever was Mrs. Turnbull's noble intention, Mitzie wanted no part of it. Had her feline intuition perceived that Mrs. Turnbull planned that she should escort Clyde to his final reward? Perhaps Mitzie's Egyptian forefathers and foremothers were okay with an unscheduled journey to the afterlife, but being a modern-day puss and not the least bit appreciative of Clyde's failed efforts to pull her off the roof, she had no intention of joining him on his voyage to the Field of Reeds. The shriek that bellowed from her moggy bosom sent chills down Agnes's spine.

A collective gasp erupted from the audience when Mitzie clawed her way up Mrs. Turnbull's suit jacket and onto her hat. Mitzie teetered on Mrs. Turnbull's hat for a moment, then vaulted off the end of Clyde's casket and onto the floor, and then plunged down the aisle toward the front door.

Mrs. Roosevelt's driver opened the front door and Mitzie was last seen heading down the block toward Wilkey's Market.

The audience shrugged and headed into the dining room to partake of the free lunch provided by the ladies of the First Church of the Evening Star and Everlasting Light.

Mrs. Odboddy – Hometown Patriot, a humorous WWII novel is available at Amazon
http://tinyurl.com/hdbvzsv

The No-Fly Zone

rowing up in Roswell, New Mexico, I heard all the stories from alien crash sites to alien autopsies in secret labs at Edwards Air Base. In my opinion, the stories are propaganda to bring in the tourists–*UFO-ers* who want to visit the site of the purported 1947 UFO crash.

Grandpa opened a bakery back in the day. Dad changed the name from Bill's Bread to The Alien Bakery in the '50s when the tourists started flooding into town, hoping for a UFO sighting and a story to tell. We specialized in artistically decorated cookies shaped like UFO space ships, the Cat from Outer Space and oval cloud cookies with a flying saucer in the center.

I took over the bakery in the '90s and brought it into the 21st century with internet cookie sales advertised on UFO blog sites and eBay. In addition to mail order, the cookies are a big hit with the tourists visiting Roswell, along with a cold drink on scorching hot summer days, and as souvenirs to take back home to disbelieving friends.

Every year, over the 4th of July weekend, only two days from now, Roswell holds a three-day UFO Festival that attracts thousands of tourists from around the world. Busloads of tourists were already flooding into town, snatching up the last motel rooms. Our seven employees were working ten-hour shifts, cutting out cookies with a cloud-punch cookie cutters, gearing up for the holiday crowds. Dad and I stayed up way past our bedtime, putting on the finishing touches of colored frosting on the cat's collar and sticking red-hot candies around the bottom of the space ship cookies.

On festival days, folks line up on the sidewalk, waiting to get through the door to buy UFO cookies. They get a kick out of Dad's original sign, still hanging over the door that reads, SHUT THE DOOR. THIS IS A NO-FLY ZONE.

Old Man Foster was a kindly old gent, blind since childhood, who ran the newspaper stand next door to the bakery. He sold papers from all over the country as well as the Roswell Daily Record and souvenir copies of the July 8, 1947 issue announcing *RAAF Captures Flying Saucer on Ranch in Roswell Region*. Of course, the story was debunked the next day when the military declared it was remnants of a weather balloon. No one bought that version and to this day, the *UFO-ers* are convinced the government covered up the story about a crashed space ship.

On his day off, Dad and Old Man Foster, both experts in astronomy, used to spend hours talking about the universe beyond our solar system. While Dad peered through a telescope, old man Foster sat in the rocking chair on our front porch, petting the cat and reading special editions of UFO magazines printed in Braille. Dad wrote articles for UFO blog sites and was often asked to speak at UFO conventions around the country, including the final evening at the conference this week.

Old Man Foster was just a child when the alleged space ship landed on his dad's ranch. Once the word got out about his relationship to *the incident*, tourists flocked to his news stand, asking him questions about his experience. Though he was always glad to talk about the solar system and possibility and probability of intelligent life in outer space, when questioned about what he'd seen on his father's ranch in 1947, he'd decline, saying that he'd never talked about it before, and he didn't intend to start now. No amount of bribes or persuasion would convince him to break his silence. He never even talked to Dad about the incident.

This morning, the temperature was already in the high 80s and it wasn't even 10:00 A.M. yet. Mirabel stood at the counter taking the orders and bagging cookies.

Jocelyn was at the cash register ringing up the sales.

Dad and I were frosting cookies. When weren't we frosting cookies day and night in the week before the festival? He commented on the number of customers we'd already served and I was about to answer when there was a commotion next door at the newspaper stand.

People waiting on the sidewalk had turned back to look.

Dad and I rushed out to check on Old Man Foster. He lay on the sidewalk, his hair matted with blood, a brick lying by his head. What was the world coming to, that someone would attack a helpless old man in broad daylight?

I called 911 and Dad knelt, pulling Old Man Foster into his lap.

He began to mumble. "Gotta' tell before I die."

Dad smoothed back his hair. "You're not going to die. What do you need to tell?"

"On the ranch, the day it crashed. Dad and I...out in the field. First a circular hole in the cloud and then it burst through, flames shooting out behind... Headed straight for us. Dad pushed me down. 'Don't look,' he yelled.

"Too late, I watched it come down...lower, lower. So bright! I put up my hand and covered my eyes. A giant flash and...and...the next thing I knew, I woke up in my room. I've been blind ever since. The next day, Dad reported it to the sheriff and the military came. Dad said they took away the thing. They told him if he talked about it, they'd put him in jail..." Mr. Foster's head rolled to the side.

"It's all right, Mr. Foster. Rest now. Help is on the way." I patted his hand, my heart in my throat. Could his story be true? Blinded by the UFO the world declared a myth?

An ambulance pulled to the curb. Two men loaded Old Man Foster into the back and roared off down the road, headed out of town.

After dinner, I called the hospital to check on him. They said Old Man Foster was never admitted. All my calls to the hospitals in neighboring counties failed to locate him. Someone said they saw the ambulance headed over toward Edwards Air Field where the secret laboratories are located, but I can't think why they'd take him there.

He's just an old man that suffered a head injury. Did someone hear him talking nonsense to Dad about a UFO that crashed in 1947? Who would believe anything he said?

Beyond the Garden Gate

fortnight ago, the sun had just begun to peak from behind the winter clouds when the child began to plead, "Let me go into the garden with my kitten." Her too-bright eyes bespoke her illness all too clear.

"Today isn't a good day to go out," I said. "There's a chill in the air. Come spring, you'll sit in the sun each day. I promise." My advice to forgo the child's dalliance in the garden fell on defiant ears, for she knew her days were numbered.

The child sighed. "Enough of this prattle. Ye' know well the thing inside my head grows each day and eats away my strength." She rubbed her eyes. "My eyes can bare see. Let me sit in the sun and write my verses if it pleasures me a little. You promised that I could go out on the next fine day."

She spoke truth and no amount of coaxing could dissuade her. How could I deny the child? Had I but prevailed that day, I might be plying her with puddings and hot chocolate today, but instead...

I bundled her with a knitted quilt, pulled her cap close upon her black curls, and tucked a pillow behind her back. She began to scribble her verses while her kitten played at her feet. His pouncing upon imaginary beasts brought a smile to her pale face. Her laughter at his antics warmed my heart.

After seeing her settled in her chair, I returned to my sewing, checking often that she wanted nothing.

Her cries brought me rushing to the garden. Not having the strength to walk, she had fallen to the grass where she lay weeping, calling her kitten's name. Between her sobs, she pointed atop the garden wall where the kit had disappeared on the other side.

With the key I carry around my waist, I unlocked the garden gate. A farmer stood most anxiously in the street, twisting his hat. "I beg pardon, nurse. 'Tweren't me fault. The kit leaped from yonder wall directly in me' 'orses' path. Betimes I cud' stop the beast, he had trod upon it. Me' apologies, miss." He hung his head. "I fear the wee thing is dead."

Hot tears pricked my eyes as I gathered the kit in my shawl. "Twas' not to be helped, sir. God speed. I'll tend the kit."

Life has dealt most unkindly to my little mistress, leaving her motherless and ill, with little to brighten her life, save the kit. Now it, too, was taken from her. I considered whether to return to the garden where my little mistress waited, or ask the gardener to hide the kit from the child.

I flew 'round the house, calling old Tom. I found him, leaning on his hoe, tending the flowers near the front door of the manse. "Tom, come here! I have great need of you!" I held the bundle toward him.

"What is t'trouble, miss? Ye' sound like... What have ye there, miss? The child's kit?"

"I fear he's jumped the wall and run afoul of horse and wagon. Bury it quickly, before she sees him. I must run to her. Even now, she lies weeping in the garden."

I ran back to the grieving child, dreading to speak of the kitten's death.

She had found the strength to rise and slouched in her chair with her tablet in her lap. Had her face not been as white as a winter snowdrift and her eyes brilliant with tears, one might not have guessed her heart was breaking. "Martha, please take me in. My hand is weary and my head hurts."

The tremble in her small voice chilled my heart. She asked no questions and I volunteered nothing. She knew the kit was dead. She took to her bed, refusing all nourishment, in spite of the favorite pudding cook brought to her bedside.

Over the next few days she declined in spirit. Though the weather was fair and I asked daily if she wished to go into the garden, she turned her face to the wall. Fearing the end must be near, I alerted the doctor of her decline following the kitten's death.

As the doctor left her room, he pressed a small vial into my hand. "This will ease her pain. Give her a spoonful when she cries out. It should last until..." What a small bottle it was.

I turned away lest he see my tears.

Cook and old Tom came often to her room. Tear-filled eyes mocked their attempts at jokes and smiles.

Two days ago, the child surprised me with improved appetite. "The sun is bright today," she said. "Will you take me to the garden?"

"It's far too cold today," I said. "You'll catch your death."

Her face twisted in a grimace as her words stabbed my heart. "What difference whether I die of cold today or another day, for surely before the first snow flies, I'll be as cold as my mother in her grave."

"I'll not hear you speak so. God rest your blessed mother. Even as you speak, your countenance brightens. Surely you're on the mend, at last."

And thus, I could not deny the child. Though a nip hung in the air, we carried her to the garden where she could lie in the sunshine and write upon her tablet.

Within an hour, hearing the creak of the gate, I hastened to the garden.

Though the chill of death was on her, the child lay as though sleeping, a smile on her lips. Though always locked and only I possess the key, the gate hung wide open...

The word of her death spread quickly through the household. Though stricken by the news, the simple message on her tablet comforts us... In a trembling hand, she wrote...

Each day in the garden, I heard my mother's voice. "Come through yon garden gate and bide with me. Heaven is beautiful this time of year."

"No," I would tell her, "I want to play with Kitten."
Last week, Kitten heard mother's call, and went over yonder wall...
Today again, I hear mother's voice. "Come. Kitten wants you to
come and bide with us."
Today, I shall go to her...

...

Even now, when I close my eyes, I see her sitting at her mother's knee, her cheeks rosy, and her kitten at her feet, chasing imaginary beasts. She looks well and happy.

Was I wrong to take her to the garden that day? Who am I to judge? Even knowing thus, should I have denied the child?

Previously published in *Inspire Promise*, 2014.

Shu-Shu's Bug

Watching my lovely Persian cats sleeping peacefully in their favorite napping spots in the living room filled me with contentment.

Shu-Shu, a silver Persian, appeared to be dozing in a sun puddle by the window, her paws tucked neatly beneath her bosom.

Honey Puff, a cream-colored Persian, napped on her favorite pillow near the patio door.

A dragonfly entered the house through a hole in the screen. It flitted momentarily across the room and landed on the arm of the sofa. It was unaware that Honey Puff had slipped from her velvet pillow and scrunched into the carpet, her ears flat, her golden eyes focused on its fluttering wings.

I could almost see the wheels turning in Honey Puff's furry little head. She was now an Instrument of Death with murder in her heart, and the dragonfly had become the enemy. She slunk across the carpet, every muscle taut, tail at half-mast.

Honey Puff inched closer, her gaze riveted on the dragonfly's iridescent wings, undulating unsuspectingly on the sofa's edge. She flexed her body and leaped. Too late. The insect had floated from the sofa, across the room and now clung to the curtain.

What ancient call of the wild wrenches the well-fed, pampered puss from her velvet pillow and turns her into a slinking tiger, stalking toward her prey?

Padding on silent, fluffy feet, Honey Puff crept toward the bug, leaped four times her height up the curtain, and executed a lethal left hook. Missing the bug again by a split second, Honey Puff dropped to the floor with a thud. Inexplicably, the dragonfly evaded the assault and fluttered aimlessly around the room.

Honey Puff's head whipped around. Where had the infernal thing gone?

Like a guided missile, she locked onto the fluttering dragonfly and followed until it settled on top of the television set; its wings thrumming to some internal rhythm.

Did the victim have any inkling that it was being stalked by a killing machine in furry gold pajamas? Who would be the victor in this battle of wits? Fascinated and amused to see how this challenge would end, I moved closer.

Honey Puff spotted her quarry on the TV and reached her target in three bounds. She stood on her back feet and thrashed at the bug; a left, a right, another left.

The wily dragonfly saw the cat's approach, raised onto gossamer wings, and took flight. This time, it landed, alas, in the sun puddle, directly in front of Shu-Shu.

The kitten spun in a circle until she spied the marauder, fluttering only a hairsbreadth from Shu-Shu's nose.

In a blink of her lovely green eyes, Shu-Shu assessed the situation. Was it too cruel to take the bug after the kitten's gallant effort to stalk the thing and bring it to its six knees? On the other hand, shouldn't one pounce when an opportunity expectedly drops literally under one's nose?

Quicker than the human eye could follow, *SWAP*! Shu-Shu's silvery paw crashed down onto the head of the dragonfly, ending its brief sojourn on earth.

Honey Puff crossed the room, her legs rigid as she approached the senior cat. She appeared disappointed that the hunt had ended so abruptly, her *stalk and kill* instinct not yet satisfied. Nevertheless, she was clearly coming to claim her prize from the elder cat. Specifically, who had connived and pursued the dragonfly to its present inglorious end? It was her bug, after all. Right? Right?

Now that the kitten was denied the pleasure of running her prey to ground and enjoying the thrill of the kill, would Shu-Shu add insult to injury and deprive her of the vanquished and squashed snack?

When Honey Puff was no less than two feet away, Shu-Shu settled the matter. She gobbled up the bug, swallowed the last wing and hind leg and burped. Whether the kitten had legitimate title to the prey was now a moot point.

I marveled at the speed with which the whole affair had transpired. A demonstration of wits and agility, an unexpected twist, a trial and execution, all within twelve seconds. Never expecting things to end quite like this, I felt sorry for the unwitting dragonfly that had had no say, whatsoever, in the decisive decision.

Honey Puff stared disgustedly at the old girl. She was definitely one peeved kitten.

Shu-Shu glared defiantly at the kitten, as if to say, "All's fair in love and bug. Get over yourself."

Then an odd thing happened. Shu-Shu's body convulsed and she chucked up the masticated bug on the rug.

Yauukk!

Shu-Shu looked at the mess of regurgitated body parts, sniffed at it, shook her long silver fur, turned and licked her right shoulder, which means in *cat-speak*, "Clearly, I assure you, the matter is of little importance and now that it's settled, I'm leaving." With a flick of her tail, she stalked from the room with the nonchalance that only a cat can pull off, even after the humiliation of disgorging an undigested dragonfly.

Honey Puff twitched her whiskers. Was that a smile? She gave the glob of wings and legs a Christian burial by scratching around it like the five points of a star, which means in *cat-speak*, "I really didn't want the skinny thing in the first place."

Sadly, this story illustrates a couple of morals.

1. From the dragonfly's point of view. Don't tempt fate by foolishly dancing within inches of certain destruction.

2. From Shu-Shu's point of view. When you attempt to profit from the efforts of a friend, you may just chuck up the whole thing on the rug.

3. From Honey Puff's point of view. Life is short. Bury your failures and live to fight another day.

The Conscientious Objector

roomtilda took me in when I was just a wee kitten. She called me Tinkleberry. *Her idea, not mine*... Over the years, as Broomtilda's health declined, it became difficult for her to find enough work around the village to buy bread and cheese. Were it not for the old cow in the byre, we would have no milk for my breakfast and Broomtilda's dinner.

One night, Broomtilda tucked her shoes under her bed, pulled the covers up to her nose and went to sleep with only milk for her dinner. Come dawn, being too weak to rise, she called me to her side. "I have provided all your needs until today, Tinkleberry. Now, you must go, my friend, kill a small beast and bring me meat, for I no longer have the means to feed us. If you fail, I shall perish."

That she should ask me to kill a living creature went against my very soul, for unlike my feline brethren, I have long been a *conscientious objector*. "You know I would do anything for you, dear Broomtilda," I said, "but to kill even the smallest living creature, I cannot do. Please do not ask me to pay such a price in return for your kindness."

"How can you answer thus, when I am ill and hungry? Have I not always provided for you?"

The tears in her eyes wrenched my heart, and yet I trembled in horror at the thought of killing even the smallest vole. "Isn't there another way to meet our needs?"

"Only one, but I dare not speak of it. It's far too dangerous," she wept.

"Whatever it might be, I shall do as you demand, if it keeps me from breaking my vow as a *conscientious objector*." I bowed my head, my hair bristling in dread.

She lifted her frail hand. "You must make your way to yonder mountain. High on the top beside a river, you'll find a cave where a wicked leprechaun dwells," she said. "Perhaps you can trick him into revealing where he hides his gold. Even if you can steal one small coin, it would feed us for many weeks. Go, now Tinkleberry. My life is in your paws, small friend." My mistress fell back upon the bed, her voice a bare whisper. "If you cannot bring back a piece of gold, our days on this earth are numbered."

I set out to do as she had bid. Though against my conscience to kill, my wits would be tested if I was to fool the evil leprechaun, steal a coin, and live to tell the tale.

The trail to the mountain was steep. With each step, I cast about in my mind how to fulfill such a task. And with each step nearer the cave, I had no clear plan how to dupe the leprechaun from his gold.

"Halt. Who goes there?" The shrill voice of the wicked leprechaun called out from beneath the log that spanned the river. "Answer, Cat, or I'll turn you to stone."

Panic seized and chilled my heart. It was now or never. An idea popped into my furry head. "I'm just a harmless little cat out for a stroll in the woods," says I. "My, what a lovely river you have here, Sir Leprechaun. I love what you've done with the place." A little honey-talk goes a long way toward soothing a malevolent spirit, or so I'm told. I sashayed across the log, humming an Irish ditty, and bowed low. "My name is Tinkleberry. *Her idea, not mine.* Pray tell, what might your name be, kind sir?"

The leprechaun's demeanor softened somewhat. "My name is Merichandrick. What do you seek?" He grumbled.

"A spot of tea would be lovely. I'm weary from my travels." I looked wistfully toward the leprechaun, hoping to convey abject vulnerability and candor. To my great relief, he invited me to step inside his abode.

"Come on in and I'll light the fire." I followed him into the grotto, aware that he might have a trick up his sleeve. Was he planning to toss me into the stew pot once inside? My nerves tingled, prepared for the worst.

"Sit over there." The imp shuffled toward the fire as I scanned the cave.

Fearing treachery, I kept one wary eye on my host as I gazed around. A green and red parrot in a cage, hung from a golden hook. "Oh, what a lovely bird," I posited, sidling closer to the cage. *Where was he hiding that blasted pot of gold?* Near the back of the cave, something lay hidden beneath a red blanket.

The little man turned. "Will you be after spending the night?" said he, with a wicked glint in his eye.

He likely plans to kill me as I lay sleeping. "If I'm so invited," says I with a yawn, patting my paw against my mouth, giving him a good view of my sharp fangs, in case he had any funny ideas. "Let us drink our tea and I'll curl up for the night just yonder on your lovely red blanket."

He shook his mop of green curls. "Not there," he shrieked, panic shining from his wicked eye. "Best you should sleep closer to the fire."

"As you wish, and I thank you kindly for the hospitality," says I. *Oho. The gold is beneath the blanket. Once the little man sleeps, I'll snatch a coin and be on my way. He'll be none the wiser from the loss of one coin.*

My host set out two mugs, poured the tea and shoved one toward me. Expecting a trick, I sneezed, and as he reached for a handkerchief, I switched the mugs. Indeed, my mug was drugged, for the evil goblin drank and fell immediately into a stupor.

As I reached to snatch a gold coin from the pot beneath the blanket, the parrot shrieked, spewing vile curses loud enough to wake the dead. Murderous rage filled my heart. Would the cursed bird ruin everything? All I needed was one small coin to save my mistress.

A *conscientious objector* no more, I leaped at the cage and knocked it to the dirt floor. The door flew open and the now repentant parrot squawked and flapped on the ground. One swift snap of my jaws, and the bird could curse no more.

Broomtilda traded the gold coin for six chickens and a second cow. Bossy gives us enough milk to sell and pay for bread and vegetables.

As a recovering *conscientious objector*, only occasionally must I venture into the woods, highjack an unsuspecting rabbit and fetch it home for the stewpot. If our fortune changes for the worse or the old cow dies, the wicked leprechaun still has a pot full of gold coins, and I know where he lives.

Joe, the Plumber

oe gripped the steering wheel and glared at the yellow Toyota ahead, crawling up the hill at thirty miles an hour. "What the heck? If we go any slower, we'll stop." He glanced at the luminous dial on his wristwatch. *8:40 A.M.* "I'm supposed to be on the job site at 8:30 A.M to pump out a septic tank. I'm going to be late."

Joe grit his teeth, shifted the truck into 2nd gear as the Toyota slowed to twenty-five mph to make the curve. He couldn't possibly pass the car. He would have to follow it all the way up the narrow crooked road.

"Crap!" Joe hit the steering wheel with his fist and then smiled in spite of himself. The expletive reminded him of his conversation with Richard last night at the local pub.

They'd had a few beers, just enough to make them both jolly. Richard cracked a few *Joe the Plumber* jokes. Everyone laughed. Then he asked the question Joe heard almost every day. "What made you start a sewage disposal service in the first place?"

Hadn't he heard that question a hundred times? It's not that they really wanted to hear the results of market survey research, the partnership offers from business associates, and incentive bank loans available to a sewage business. The jerk had already made up his mind, and added, "Isn't that a crappy career choice… No pun intended. *Heh. Heh.*"

"Well, it's this way…" He'd kept as straight a face as he could muster. "When I was a kid, my mother tried every trick in the book to get me potty-trained, but I resisted everything she tried. Nothing worked. Not punishments, rewards or stars on the blackboard. Not until I made up my mind to do it myself.

"Over the years, she told the story so often, it was in the back of my mind and suggested a career choice. So I started my septic business and called it *The Pooper Scooper*. Does that answer your question?"

Richard had seemed shaken by the story. Then he must have realized Joe was making a joke. Richard blushed and excused himself, saying he needed to use the john, but he never came back. He probably slipped out the back door.

Joe filed the conversation away in his head. He vowed to tell it again the next time someone asked the same stupid question. It was a tossup which he'd heard more, 'Joe the Plumber' jokes or questions about his choice of such a 'crappy business'.

At the top of the hill, the Toyota finally turned off into a side road. Joe shifted his truck back into 3rd gear and stepped on the gas. Old Pooper's gears squealed and lunged forward.

Within ten minutes, he was at the job site. He opened the truck door and jumped out, nearly stepping on an orange tabby cat's tail. "Sorry, kitty. Didn't see you there." He turned as the screen door opened and a skinny guy with long hair and a three-day beard stepped out.

Skinny Guy shifted from one foot to the other as Joe flipped dials on the side of the truck. "Sorry, I'm late. I got held up in traffic. So, where's the tank?"

"*Um*, well, man, I guess it's over there somewhere." Skinny Guy pointed in the direction of a building sitting toward the back of the lot.

The paint on the side of the building was peeling, and boards nailed loosely across the window suggested it had been abandoned for years. A shiny new padlock was attached to the doorknob. *That's quite a padlock on an old building like that.* Joe shrugged and returned to the business at hand, removing the equipment needed to locate the site of the septic tank.

For the next twenty minutes, Joe worked with his metal detector until he discovered the sewer pipe and followed it to the tank while the tabby cat followed his progress. Joe made small talk with the cat as he probed the ground and finding the location of the tank, dug down a foot to uncover the lid. He turned gauges on the side of the truck, inserted the hose into the septic tank, and started the pumping process.

Skinny Guy stood around for a while and then went into the house. Once the hoses were connected, it became a waiting game. There wasn't much to do for the next thirty minutes or so except monitor the gauges on the truck. Joe liked to play a mind-association game while he waited, trying to guess his client's favorite sport or hobby. It wasn't hard. Usually, there was something in the yard or around the house that told the story.

Last week, the client had a golf cart parked by the side of the house. That was a dead giveaway. Or the guy with the antlers nailed above the garage door. Mighty hunter type. Or the guy with the row of roses, trimmed like House Beautiful. It was mind-candy, but it gave him something to think about while he waited for Old Pooper to do its job.

Joe hitched his belt over the spare tire he carried around his belly. He gazed around the yard. *So what turns Skinny Guy on?* From the attentions of the friendly cat, it looked like Skinny Guy was into animals. It sure wasn't a House Beautiful concept. The place was a mess. Tin cans and bottles lay in heaps. Old cardboard boxes stacked up by the old building crumbled in the sun.

The yard was two-feet deep with weeds, except for the worn path leading from the house to the old building with the padlock. *That's odd. Now, why the heck would he do that?*

Old Pooper slurped and gurgled. Almost done. It wouldn't be long now, and he'd have to knock on the door and ask for a check. In the meantime…*Wait a minute*. Joe sniffed. Something wasn't right. After several years of pumping septic tanks, he'd gotten used to the stink. Septic tanks never smelled good, but this one smelled even worse, like chemicals or something. *Just what is in that old building?* A thin thread of steam curled upward from a vent pipe in the roof. The hairs raised on the back of his neck.

Joe ambled toward the old building, looking over his shoulder. The TV blared inside the house. Skinny Guy was still in there.

Joe stood near the run-down shed beside the boarded-up window. He lit a cigarette, took a puff and leaned against the wall, trying to look the picture of innocence. *Can't see through the boards.* He glanced around the yard. *No one in sight.*

Old Pooper chugged in the background. Joe pulled a screwdriver from his overalls pocket and pried at the nails on the top board, glancing from time to time over his shoulder at the house. Nothing stirred. The board squeaked as the nails came loose, and dropped down a couple of inches. Shielding his eyes with his hands, he peeked through a crack in the window. *What the heck?*

Cupboards lined the walls. Beakers, tubes, and vials covered the countertop. The sink was piled high with bottles and bowls. Add all this to the smell seeping from the septic tank... *A meth lab.*

"What the heck are you looking at?"

Startled, Joe jumped. He turned.

Skinny Guy stood just outside his back door, fists clenched; his mouth pulled down in a scowl.

Joe's stomach flipped over and back again. *Did he see me pull the board off the window?* Joe searched for an answer. "Hey, man! It's cool. I thought there might be a john inside. All that smell has turned my stomach."

Skinny Guy wasn't buying his story. He reached back and pulled a pistol from behind his waistband. "Shut up and step away from the building." A dribble of spittle flew from his mouth with each syllable.

Joe put up his hands. "Take it easy with that thing. I'm comin'." He moved toward the truck.

"Get on in there. I gotta' figure out..." Skinny Guy growled, jerking his gun toward the house.

Old Pooper sputtered and gurgled, nearing the bottom of the septic tank. Joe took a step closer to the truck. "Gimme a second. This thing's about done. Can I just turn it off?"

Without waiting for an answer, he reached toward the dials and flipped the red reverse switch on the instrument panel that started the sucking process. He grabbed the hose and yanked it out of the septic tank. Driven by the pressure inside Old Pooper, the hose whipped and skittered across the ground, spewing the tank's contents from the end of the tube. Green slime struck Skinny Guy, knocked him to his knees, splashed across his body and into his face. The gun flew from his hand and landed in the tall grass. He shrieked and clawed at his face.

Joe leaped forward, picked up the gun, grabbed Skinny Guy by the collar, and yanked him to his feet.

The man pulled at his clothing, spitting the foul green stuff, and flailing his arms until he stood naked in the weeds, shaking and crying. With streaks of greenish-brown slime still smeared on his body, he looked like a moldy gingerbread boy.

Joe flipped Old Pooper's levers and turned off the pumps. He used his mobile device to call his office. "Hey, yeah, this is Joe. I'm out on a job on Lakeville Road. There's a meth lab here on the property in one of the outbuildings. Can you call the cops and have them send out a patrol car?

"Everything's under control. By the way, would you ask the cops to bring along a cardboard box"?

"*Uh huh…*"

"What? Why? Because, I'm bringing home a cat."

The Salami Caper

It was a dark and windy night—April, 1865. A man swathed in black creeps down the hall, looks back, and then thrusts a derringer beneath the folds of his long, dark cape. Perspiration dots his forehead as he approaches President Lincoln's private box. His hand trembles. He turns the doorknob.

"A black, gloved hand holding a gun inches through the door. Inside the theater, the audience laughs uproariously in the third act. The assassin takes careful aim at the President's head and squeezes the trigger."

The thundering voice resonates through the shadowy corridors as it continues its description of that fateful night. "Tonight is April 15, 1865. All things are as they were then, except YOU ARE THERE!"

BANG!

A stand of lights aimed at the actors re-enacting the popular 1953 television show crashes to the floor.

"Cut! Cut!" Byron, the director, heaves his cumbersome body from the director's chair and glares at the lighting technician.

Fourteen heads swivel toward the youth, stooping to pick up the lampstand.

"Sorry! I stumbled over the cat. Won't happen again." The youth glances nervously at the shattered glass covering the floor and then glares at Humphrey, one of the studio's resident mousers.

Humphrey scurries off the set.

Byron checks his watch, raises his hand, and strides toward the distinguished actor playing Mr. Lincoln. "Oh, Martin. A moment? The costume department is bringing you another top hat. Yours is looking pretty shabby." He advances toward the older, distinguished actor seated in the theater box.

Martin jumps to his feet, stammering, "Oh…I don't think…" His cheeks turn rosy red.

"What's wrong? Is there a problem?"

Martin shakes his head. "Not at all. Here you go." He hands the hat to Byron.

"Don't worry. We'll have another brought from Props right after lunch." Byron claps, "One hour for lunch. We shoot at 2:20 P.M."

Cast and crew, technicians, make-up and hairdressers all move toward the outside studio door, chattering.

Byron sets Martin's hat on the edge of the buffet table, picks up his clipboard and begins to make changes to the script.

Humphrey, a brown tabby and Marilyn, a long-haired cream, creep toward the unattended buffet table where the crew will dine at the end of today's shoot. Humphrey stands on his hind feet, twitching his nose toward a plate of gourmet salami and cheese balls. Beside the platter is a large roll of unsliced Rosette de Lyon 'Fiore' salami, aged to perfection in its white powdery casing. Humphrey raises a tentative claw, and snags the edge of the plate. Salami and meatballs hit the floor. *Splat!*

"Scat!" Byron shoos away the cats, kneels and scoops up the scattered *hors do oeuvres*.

Humphrey scampers under the table with a pilfered meatball.

Byron glances up just as a gloved hand snatches the top hat from the table and…*Wham!* Dazed by a blow to the head, he topples to the floor. The roll of salami rolls under the table.

"He's coming around. Bring me more ice." Martin holds a wet cloth to Byron's head.

A crew member picks up the heavy salami roll and starts to return it to the table.

"Leave it there," Martin says. "That's likely what the perpetrator used to whack him in the head. There might be fingerprints." Martin presses the ice pack to the rising lump on Byron's head. "Someone call 911."

"No. No police." Byron struggles to sit up. "I'll be fine. We don't need the publicity. Sponsors don't like bad press."

A cast member speaks from the back of the studio. "Aren't they shooting Columbo at the studio next door?" Fourteen heads swivel toward the absurd suggestion. Never mind that Martin has suffered a real assault, not a made-for-TV series. Never mind that the weapon was likely an aged salami. Never mind that Columbo is a make-believe detective. Fourteen heads nod in agreement. "Good idea. He's our man. He can solve it. Let's give him a call."

The recruited actor who plays the TV detective, Columbo, fixes one eye on Byron, while the other roves the room with wild abandon. "Your attacker is indubitably someone on the set. What happened?"

"I set Mr. Lincoln's hat on the table and the next thing I know, I'm on the floor." Byron says.

"Can you describe the perpetrator who struck you with the alleged salami?" *Columbo* stares daggers at the crew.

"All I saw was a dark figure—maybe wearing a dark cape?" Byron answers.

The cast turns toward Charles, the actor playing John Wilkes Booth, whose chosen attire during the scene was, indeed, a black cape.

"It wasn't me," says Charles. "I left my cape on the coat rack when I went to lunch. I was with Martin the entire time we were off the set. Tell him, Martin."

Martin nods, giving Marilyn a scratch behind her jeweled collar.

Heads swivel back to Columbo. He casts his good eye over the crowd and shoves his hands in his raincoat pocket. "Did any of the suspects leave the cafeteria during the lunch hour?"

Charles glares at Melville, the actor who plays the part of Henry Rathbone, Mr. Lincoln's theater companion on the night of the murder. "Melville auditioned for John Wilkes Booth's role. He was mad at Byron because he didn't get the part." Charles points toward Melville, the newly accused. "I saw him leave the cafeteria."

All eyes shift to Melville. "It wasn't me." Melville gestures toward Byron's wife, the actress who plays the role of Lincoln's wife, and also bears her name. "I met Mary at lunch to give her a down payment. I'm buying her old Mercedes."

Mary nods.

Heads twist back to the rumpled detective. He scratches his head. "Let me cogitate a minute." He snaps his fingers and smiles. "Oh, one more thing…Where is Mr. Lincoln's hat?"

Byron and the crew gaze toward the buffet table. The hat was gone.

Columbo shrugs, rubs his hands over his chin. "The attacker wasn't after Byron, per se. He was after Mr. Lincoln's hat."

Fourteen actors turn questioning eyes toward Martin, who plays Mr. Lincoln. He shifts from foot to foot. His face pinks up. "It wasn't me. I'm an actor, not a hat fancier."

Meow. Meow.

The crew turns toward Claudia, the pretty make-up artist. She flaps her hands at the cats, noses a-twitch, reaching up her legs. "*Shoo. Shoo.* Get away from me."

Humphrey paws and sniffs her arm and utters a plaintive, *mew-mew.*

Fourteen mouths gasp in disbelief, recognizing the white powdery substance clinging to Claudia's wrist as the *fiore* from the salami, the presumed weapon used against Byron's noggin.

"Look. Humphrey's solved the crime. Claudia? Why did you do it?" Martin rushes toward her, then stops. He turns back to his wife, puts up his hands and shakes his head. "Mary, I'm sorry. Claudia never meant anything to me. You know I love only you, *charisma, mi amore…*"

Claudia crumples to the floor, sobbing. "Martin, darling. You forced me to do it. I couldn't wait any longer. You promised to divorce Mary. I put another letter in your hat this morning, like every morning. But, not a love letter this time. I threatened to tell the tabloids about us if you didn't divorce your wife. Byron was sending your hat to Props. I couldn't let them find my letter. You can see why I had to get the hat back and protect our love. I did it for us, darling."

"Case closed. Will someone call the police?" Columbo casts a wayward eye across the set, grinning at nobody in particular. "If you'll excuse me, I've got a whole crew next door sitting on their hands costing me time-and-a-half." He heads for the door. "Oh, one more thing. My agent will send over a bill for my time."

The police arrive, handcuff Claudia and arrest her for *assault with a deadly salami.*

The crew members gather around the buffet table and fill their plates with cheese and salami. Mary pours wine into each long-stemmed plastic flute. She lifts her glass. "To Claudia. If only she'd waited another few days. I'm divorcing Martin. I filed the paperwork last week."

Tch. Tch. Fourteen heads nod and lift their glass. "Poor Claudia!"

Why, Master, Why?

aster brought home a dog a week ago. It was obvious that liked the dog better than me, but I didn't mind. Some men like dogs better than cats. I could live with that. I understood.

Last night, Master came upon me napping in the yard, grabbed me, and dropped me in a sack. He tossed me into the back seat of his car. My heart was in my throat. I shook with fear as the car rumbled. After a while, the car stopped and the bag lifted. Though I didn't understand what was happening, I was sure there must be a good reason. I trusted Master to take care of me.

The next thing I knew, the sack was soaring through the air and I landed with a thump. Something hard rammed into my ribs, almost knocking the breath from me. I lay in the dark sack for a minute, confused and stunned. Something terrible must have happened? Was it a car accident? Surely, Master would rescue me. Then I heard our car rumbling away and then, silence. *Why, Master, Why? Why didn't you save me? Why have you deserted me?*

Despite the pain in my ribs, I fought my way free from the sack and crawled into the dark night. Cold air struck my face and stabbed through my lungs.

Why had this happened? I always tried to be the kind of kitty he wanted. I always ate my dinner, even when he put scraps from his plate into my dish. I always used my litter box, even when it wasn't very clean. Didn't I keep his barn free of mice? I was careful not to sleep on his shirt, even though it smelled of him, and I wanted to be near him.

He threw me away on a dark country road like a bag of garbage. My heart hardened against him. I will never understand this. My shoulder hurt, but my heart is broken. I can never go home even if I knew which way to go. I was alone, cold, hungry, and scared. I walked all night, lost in thought.

When the Great Creator gave man dominion over the animals, He intended there should be a kinship between us. Master's job was to protect and mine was to serve. I held up my end of the bargain. Didn't I chase the crows from his field? Didn't I always come when he called? Master was wrong to do me this way. My heart is full of rage. I will never forgive him.

When the sun came up this morning, I stopped in a Eucalyptus grove and lay in the shrubbery to rest beneath the trees. A soft breeze whispered a hypnotic melody through the leaves, and I slept. In sleep, there is no pain, no bitterness, only sweet relief.

I awoke refreshed at midday, but resentment filled my heart.

Hunger pangs gnawed at my belly. Across the field, I saw a tiny yellow house. A child's swing hung from a nearby willow tree, and flowers bloomed beside the kitchen door. It was the kind of house where a kind person might live, a person who might give me a piece of bread and a drink of milk.

I crept along the grass, stopping every little while to listen and sniff. The perfume of honeysuckle and roses scented the air. A child laughed and a baby cooed in response to a woman's lullaby. The love inside the little yellow house sneaked beneath the door and stole across the yard. It swept over me like a soft breeze, ruffled the fur on my back and seeped into my soul. My heart yearned to belong, to have a loving family like this.

The door opened. I hunkered in the grass, shaking with fear, still tingling from the energy of love swirling around the yard. I stared fearfully into the woman's eyes. Would she reject me, too?

The woman stooped, ready to gather me into her arms. "Hello, kitty. Are you hungry? Do you want to come inside? "

I trembled as a battle raged within my breast. How I wished to be held and loved by this woman, but my heart was filled with bitterness.

Love and hate cannot dwell in the same space. If I couldn't let go of my anger and forgive Master for his betrayal, how could I remain in the presence of such love? "Oh, Great Creator, when You created the creatures of the world, You must have put a bit of Your ability to forgive into each of us. Help me find the strength to forgive so that I might remain in this home forever."

The mother smiled and knelt. "Poor kitty. Are you lost?" She stroked my head.

In that moment, I knew God heard my prayer. In her caress, I felt the touch of God and with that touch, all bitterness toward Master fell away. With my heart singing, I leaped into her arms, ready to begin a new life.

Meeting Noe-Noe

Meeting Noe-Noe is an edited excerpt from my cozy cat mystery novel, **Black Cat and the Lethal Lawyer**. *It takes place on a horse ranch in Texas near the Mexican border. Thumper has come to the horse ranch and sees Grandmother's cat for the first time.*

With four white feet tucked beneath his belly and his fluffy black tail whipping, Thumper peeked out from beneath the sofa. He heard Brett and Kimberlee's voices out on the patio. He sniffed, savoring the unfamiliar smells of hay and horses drifting through the open window of Grandma Lassiter's ranch house. Another delightful scent wafted across the room and sneaked beneath his hiding place, teasing his nostrils and making the hair on the back of his neck stand erect. The scent tasted familiar and yet…evocative and foreign.

Oh, moment of discovery, sweet love's fantasy revealed. He poked his head from beneath the sofa and lifted his nose, drew in the bouquet, rolled it around his tongue and teeth, seeking to identify the direction of the tantalizing bouquet. After several long minutes, he crept from his hiding place and followed the enticing aroma. *Aha. The flavor of a feminine flower, not a figment of my furtive fantasy.*

She drew him as if by magic—teasing, taunting, beguiling him until his senses reeled. He padded through the house, but to his dismay was unable to locate this unseen temptress, this invisible goddess, this captivating illusion that occupied his mind.

He followed the fragrance into the library, his gaze traveling up the bookcases where he spied Lillian Braun's *Cat Who* series and a complete collection of *Rita May Brown and Sneaky Pie Brown.* Kimberlee often displayed the titles in her bookstore window, examples of inspired modern day mysteries for ailurophiles.

Their eyes met as the fascinating creature peered down from the top of the bookshelf, her front toes curled beneath her breast. The sun streaming through the window shimmered off her silken ears. Her fur, like rows of buttercups set in a field of marigolds, shot through a summer sunset. Her eyes, midnight slits peeking through golden moons. Her sensuous tail coiled around her nose, rising and falling in a hypnotic rhythm, matching the thud of his heart.

Electricity crackled through the library. She was not a gossamer dream, but a lissome feline goddess. She stared down from atop the shelf with total insouciance—a living, breathing, challenge to his masterful art of *woomanship.*

During his bachelor days at Fern Lake, he had always preferred a darker-furred girlfriend as opposed to the lighter tabby-marked variety. His interest in this golden-haired vixen with stripes the color of marigolds was both perplexing and titillating.

He'd had his share of lady friends, though he was not obsessed with romance. He fancied himself a diplomatic lover, not given to one-night stands, but more discerning in his treatment of female companions. He disliked the idea of *love em' and leave em',* having heard tales of his father's abandonment issues following mother's whirlwind romance. Mother had shared stories of her lonely nights on the fencepost, waiting in vain for his father's return. Thumper vowed he wouldn't be that kind of cat or cad. But, this enticing, exotic creature was something a cat could sink his teeth into. This lady begged a more committed long-term relationship.

Now, to put his best foot forward–but which foot? All four of his nimble black legs ended in elegant, snowy white feet with multiple toes. He stretched out his front legs, raised his rear to display his muscular posterior and tight gluts. He then twisted into a three-point pretzel-like position and licked his inner thighs. These contortions were calculated to demonstrate his strongest attributes and yet reveal a willingness to concede control, a maneuver that he had perfected. It had never failed in his effort to impress a lady cat yet.

"Howdy, stranger. New in town?" The sound of her voice, like the thrum of a hummingbird's wings, sent shockwaves through his heart.

He stared into her enchanting face—the angle of her teasing whiskers—the slant of taunting ears—her tantalizing eyes, tinged ever so slightly with green, glittered in the sunlight. Her tiny pointed teeth—perfection.

She breathed a sigh and twitched her tail in a seductive manner.

Okay, you're up, Thumper. Remember, you don't get a second chance to make a first impression. "Thumper's the name. Brought the family to visit the grandmother for a few days. Care to show me around?" He licked his bib into a conflate of black and white, turned and stared out the window. "Not that it matters one way or the other if you do or don't, you understand. Just sayin'." *Please say yes, oh please, please, say yes…*

"Thumper? What kind of name is that? Sounds like a rabbit."

His heart crumpled at the disdain in her voice. There it was again, that silly name. Thumper—like the bunny. How many times had he wished that Amanda would have named him Butch or Cruncher. Or even Felix. But no—since Kimberlee came into his life, he had to go through life as—Thumper. His dream of a romantic fling with this straw-colored vixen had as much chance now as a balloon at a porcupine's birthday party. He sighed.

Might as well leave before things get ugly. With hanging head, he shuffled to the door.

"Wait." The sound of her velvet voice stopped him. With ears perked and whiskers taunt, he glanced back. "Yes?"

She stood and rearranged her sumptuous body on the top shelf. No question. All her curves were in the right places. "Don't go yet, Thumper. I like rabbits."

Hallelujah! Hallelujah!

Black Cat and the Lethal Lawyer is available at Amazon.com
(e-book $3.99)
http://tinyurl.com/q3qrgyu

Also by Elaine

Black Cat's Mysteries

Black Cat's Legacy

Elaine Faber

Black Cat's Legacy

A tale of intrigue and murder with a touch of whimsy.

Thumper, the resident Fern Lake black cat, knows where the bodies are buried and it's up to Kimberlee to decode the clues.

Kimberlee's arrival at the Fern Lake lodge triggers the Black Cat's Legacy. With the aid of his ancestors' memories, it's Thumper's duty to guide Kimberlee to clues that can help solve her father's cold case murder. She joins forces with a local homicide detective and an author, also researching the murder for his next thriller novel. As the investigation ensues, Kimberlee learns more than she wants to know about her father. The murder suspects multiply, some dead and some still very much alive, but someone at the lodge will stop at nothing to hide the Fern Lake mysteries.

Available at Amazon: http://tinyurl.com/lrvevgm

Cover photo *Boot's Eyes*: © Elaine Faber

Black Cat and the Lethal Lawyer

With the promise to name a beneficiary to her multi-million dollar horse ranch, Kimberlee's grandmother entices her and her family to Texas. But things are not as they appear and Thumper, the black cat with superior intellect, uncovers the appalling reason for the invitation. Kimberlee and Brett discover a fake Children's Benefit Program and the possible false identity of the stable master. To make matters worse,

Thumper overhears a murder plot, and he and his newly found soul-mate, Noe-Noe, must do battle with a killer to save Grandmother's life.

The further Kimberlee and her family delve into things, the deeper they are thrust into a web of embezzlement, greed, vicious lies and murder. With the aid of his ancestors' memories, Thumper unravels some dark mysteries. Is it best to reveal the past or should some secrets never be told?

Elaine Faber

Black Cat and the Lethal Lawyer

A tale of betrayal and greed with a splash of fantasy.

Available at Amazon: http://tinyurl.com/lg7yvgq

Elaine Faber

Black Cat
and the
Accidental Angel

A tale of memories lost and love found with a touch of the divine.

When the family SUV flips and Kimberlee is rushed to the hospital, Black Cat (Thumper) and his soulmate are left behind. Black Cat loses all memory of his former life and the identity of the lovely feline companion by his side. "Call me Angel. I'm here to take care of you." Her words set them on a long journey toward home, and life brings them face to face with episodes of joy and sorrow.

The two cats are taken in by John and his young daughter, Cindy, facing foreclosure of the family vineyard and emu farm. In addition, someone is playing increasingly dangerous pranks that threaten Cindy's safety. Angel makes it her mission to help their new family. She puts her life at risk to protect the child, and Black Cat learns there are more important things than knowing your real name.

Elaine Faber's e-books are available on Amazon for $3.99. Print books. $16.00. http://tinyurl.com/07zcsm2

Cover photo *Black and White Cat*: © vivienstock, http://us.fotolia.com/id/46333972 (halo added)

Mrs. Odboddy Series

Mrs. Odboddy: Hometown Patriot

Since the onset of WWII, Agnes Agatha Odboddy, hometown patriot and self-appointed scourge of the underworld, suspects conspiracies around every corner…stolen ration books, German spies running amuck, and a possible Japanese invasion off the California coast. This seventy-year-old, model citizen would set the world aright if she could get Chief Waddlemucker to pay attention to the town's nefarious deeds on any given Meatless Monday.

Mrs. Odboddy vows to bring the villains, both foreign and domestic, to justice, all while keeping chickens in her bathroom, working at the Ration Stamp Office, and knitting argyles for the boys on the front lines.

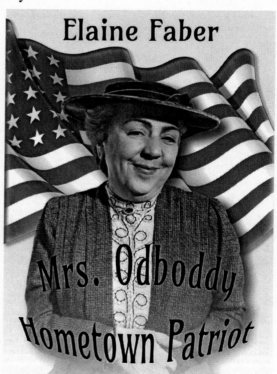

Imagine the chaos when Agnes's long-lost WWI lover returns, hoping to find a million dollars in missing Hawaiian money and rekindle their ancient romance. In the thrilling conclusion, Agnes's predictions become all too real when Mrs. Roosevelt unexpectedly comes to town to attend a funeral and Agnes must prove that she is, indeed, a warrior on the home front.

Elaine Faber

Mrs. Odboddy Hometown Patriot

A WWII tale of chicks and chicanery, suspicion and spies.

Find Mrs. Odboddy on Amazon: http://tinyrul.com/hdbvzsv

Cover photos: Shutterstock.com images 227271556 and 148131515

Asked to accompany Mrs. Roosevelt on her Pacific Island tour, Agnes and Katherine travel by train to Washington, D.C. Agnes carries a package for Colonel Farthingworth to President Roosevelt.

A WWII tale of mystery, mischief, and mishaps.

Convinced the package contains secret war documents, Agnes expects Nazi spies to try and derail her mission.

She meets Irving, whose wife mysteriously disappears from the train; Nanny, the unfeeling caregiver to little Madeline; two soldiers bound for training as Tuskegee airmen; and Charles, the shell-shocked veteran, who lends an unexpected helping hand. Who will Agnes trust? Who is the Nazi spy?

When enemy forces make a final attempt to steal the package in Washington, D.C., Agnes must accept her own vulnerability as a warrior on the home front.

Can Agnes overcome multiple obstacles, deliver the package to the President, and still meet Mrs. Roosevelt's plane before she leaves for the Pacific Islands?

Available on Amazon: http://tinyurl/com/jn5bzwb

Coming Soon:

Mrs. Odboddy: And Then There Was a Tiger

While the tiger of war wages over Europe and in the Pacific during late fall, 1943, elderly, eccentric, Mrs. Odboddy and her granddaughter, Katherine, fight the war from the home front and face their own *tigers*.

Framed for a crime and ostracized by the townsfolk, Agnes is hard pressed to keep up her spirits and deal with the return of her *on-again, off-again* World War One lover, Godfrey Baumgarten.

Katherine confronts her own *tigers* when a tug-a-war ensues for her affections, definitely endangering her engagement to Dr. Don Dew-Right.

Then a traveling carnival comes to town with a real, live tiger, and counterfeit bills appear in Katherine's dessert booth. $200 collected from the sale of War Bonds goes astray on Agnes's watch.

Determined to resolve the matter before the loss of the money is discovered and she is accused of yet another crime, Mrs. Odboddy sets out alone to find the missing cash. Of course, her bumbling uncovers a criminal gang and her life is in danger, unless she outwits the scoundrels who exploit the chaos of war to their own advantage.

Special Thanks

Thanks to the encouragement of my children, Londa Faber and Michael Faber, I present this assortment of short cat stories for your reading enjoyment.

Thanks to my husband, Leland Faber, for his patience and willingness to stop everything and listen, and lend suggestions and advice when I have questions about technical issues.

Thanks to my beta readers, Lois Parrish and Erin Bambery-Veliquette.

Thanks to my fans who ask, "When are you publishing the next one?" Your encouragement keeps me writing.

Special thanks to my mentor and friend, Julie Williams, for her expert assistance along my writing journey.

Thanks to the Lord Jesus Christs, for every good thing and for the ability to write the stories that continue to entertain my readers.

CPSIA information can be obtained
at www.ICGtesting.com
Printed in the USA
FSOW01n0142291217
42465FS